SEAN
YEAGER

and the DNA Thief

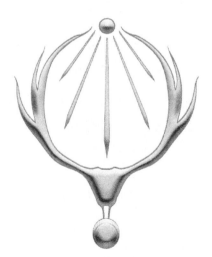

D. M. JARRETT

For more information about titles in the Sean Yeager Adventures series visit: www.SeanYeager.com

Sean Yeager returns in:
Sean Yeager **Hunters Hunted**

Available (in sequence):
Sean Yeager and the DNA Thief
Sean Yeager Hunters Hunted
Sean Yeager Claws of Time
Sean Yeager Mortal Thread

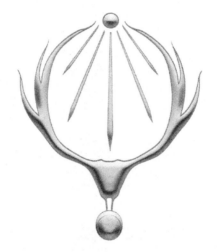

SEAN YEAGER
and the DNA Thief

Sean Yeager is a determined teenager drawn into an ancient and perilous struggle. Following an unexplained burglary, Sean's life is turned upside down when he discovers enemies and abilities he never knew he had. He is protected by a mysterious organisation called the Foundation, but can they be trusted, and are they as formidable as they appear? Sean tries to recover his most prized possessions and searches for clues about his missing father, if he can survive long enough.

Fourth UK edition

This edition published by Aenathen Omega.
www.SeanYeager.com

This edition first published in 2021.
First published in 2012.

A CIP catalogue record for this book is available from the British Library.

ISBN 9781093560879

For adventurers young and old.

With grateful thanks and appreciation to Sean, Mary, and Freddie.

.

CONTENTS

CHAPTER 1: ALERT

It was a bright, sunny day. Between showers, it was refreshing and warm. Beneath them, it was like being assaulted by a power washer. Steam rose from the pavements, and passers-by darted between rain shelters. Sinister clouds loomed overhead, and another deluge was due at any moment.

Sean Yeager and his mother, Sarah, arrived home after a tedious shopping trip. The regular stores had sold out of grey school trousers, but Sean was elated at the prospect of being unable to return to school. Mrs Yeager was less than impressed, grumpy even. She glanced in the rear-view mirror, threw back her long blonde hair, and let out a silent scream. Her day had unravelled into a mess, and her roots were in dire need of attention. As for her wardrobe, she was still making do with last year's clothes, which were now threadbare. Mrs Yeager consoled herself that at least she had managed to regain her trim figure, thanks to park runs and the slimming club. But what about Sean's school uniform? Where on Earth could she find three pairs of grey trousers in only two days?

Mrs Yeager parked her battered family car and alighted on the driveway outside their house. It was a humble, red brick dwelling in a small English town, but it was home. Car doors clunked, and keys rattled in the front door to sighs of relief all around. A *welcome* doormat invited them inside to a faint smell of baking and fingerprint-marked wallpaper. All that was missing was a dog. They were forbidden according to a shambolic man from the Foundation who dropped by whenever it suited him. He had mumbled something about digging up bugs or insects Mrs Yeager was unsure which.

Sean's father was still missing, presumed lost on a classified Foundation mission. Although Sean had not seen him since he was three, he would often ask about his father. Whenever Sean demanded to know what had become of his father, it brought tears to Mrs Yeager's eyes. It was bad enough that his father was missing. Worse, Mrs Yeager had no idea if he was still alive. As for the much-wanted dog, they had resorted to borrowing other people's pets from time to time. It had felt strange at first, but returning them without drama or expense was a definite bonus.

Sean was an inquisitive and restless teenager. He lived a normal life in an unremarkable town and attended a mundane, yet slightly eccentric senior school. Sean was tall for his age and good at sport when he chose to be. Although, he preferred to keep his mind active. Sean was an only child and, outside of school, he liked to play strategy games on his computer. His favourite was *Conquest of the Vuloz*, a galactic campaign with real-time battles.

In an unguarded moment, Sean's thoughts returned to school, and he winced. The prospect of sitting through hours of boring lessons was not appealing, but he looked forward to seeing his school friends again. Sean wondered where they had been during the long summer holidays. Perhaps they had travelled overseas, visiting new countries? Something Sean was denied for reasons never properly explained to him.

'Have you seen my phone anywhere?' said Mrs Yeager, hanging up her raincoat. 'I could have sworn I left it on the table.'

'Perhaps some aliens took it?' said Sean, slumping full-length on a faded sofa in the living room.

'They came all this way *just* to steal my phone?' said Mrs Yeager, scouring the room.

'Yeah, they're invisible. They landed in the back garden, didn't you know?' said Sean, rising to join the search.

'They'd better not phone home,' said Mrs Yeager. 'Not on *my* tariff.'

Sean stood bolt upright in the middle of the living room. He tensed, and veins in his neck began to throb.

'*Where* is my Dreampad?'

'I don't know, Sean. Have you tried looking for it?'

'Have you hidden it again?'

'No, of course not. Have you checked your room?' said Mrs Yeager.

In truth, she wished aliens *had* broken in and stolen the Dreampad. Not her phone. That was much too important. But if a game kept him busy, where was the harm? On second thoughts, it would be better if aliens *had* found his Dreampad. Better still if they had thrown it into a black hole on *Conquest of the Nerdwasters* or whatever it was called. Perhaps then Sean would focus on his homework and behave like a normal human being?

'He's just like his father,' she thought. 'Always tinkering around with gadgets. Right, *phone*, where are you? Sean, help me look for it, will you?'

Her plea hung in the air unanswered because Sean was gone.

Sean charged upstairs like a hungry bear pursuing a hiker up a hill. He flung open his bedroom door and dived under the bed. But the carpet was dusty and bare.

'Where are my crates?' he cried, his heart racing.

The only sign of his cherished possessions were rows of dirty grooves in the carpet. His Dreampad and charger were gone. His books were gone. His prized collection of comics and model cars had vanished. Even *Rise of the Ultrabulous One*, a rare collector's edition given to him by his father, was gone. Sean let out a snarl. His heart began to pound.

'If Mum's taken my stuff!'

'What's all the fuss about?' said Mrs Yeager, joining him.

'Where are my crates?' said Sean. 'You've taken them, haven't you?'

'You know I would never take your...'

Mrs Yeager's lower lip quivered in mid-sentence. She stood motionless and stared at the wall. Sean followed her gaze. Above the bed was a large circular hole where the bedroom wall should have been. It was like a perfect round window without a frame or glass. Around its edges, the bricks and plaster had been cut clean through to reveal yellow fluffs of insulation. Sean froze. He watched people walk up and down the pavement holding umbrellas at the ready. In the distance, a black cat tiptoed across the road to avoid the puddles. He shook his head.

'Where are my posters? What happened to the wall?'

'I'm calling the Police,' said Mrs Yeager. 'This is the last straw.'

Sean crawled across the bed and craned his neck through the hole, hoping to find his belongings on the ground. He felt a breeze on his face and a warm flash of sunlight.

'Sean! Get away from there!' said Mrs Yeager.

Sean felt himself being dragged back by his ankles, and the duvet ruffled beneath him.

'They've taken all my stuff! How am I going to play games? How am I going to talk to my friends? How am I going to have any *fun*?'

'It's okay, Sean. We can replace them,' said Mrs Yeager, attempting a clumsy embrace.

Sean wriggled free.

'You don't understand! No one understands! Dad left me those comics. They're all I have left,' said Sean, with tears running down his face.

Apart from a handful of photographs, Sean had no connection with his father. He could vaguely remember meeting him and felt an emptiness inside. Sean wanted to know what his father was like and to spend time with him. He had tried asking his mother, but she usually broke down in tears. In the end, Sean gave up and turned to his comics and games for solace. He imagined his father was an action hero who had saved a whole town but was unable to save himself. It was a tragic version of events, but it made him feel slightly better.

Daylight turned to dusk, and there was a sharp crack of thunder followed by a sheet of rain. The sudden downpour was like someone had opened a bath tap in the sky. A few specks of water blew sideways and settled on Sean's face. In horror, he dragged his mother from the bedroom and slammed the door behind them.

'I bet it was that Foundation mob,' said Mrs Yeager.'

She wandered off and returned with a telephone handset on loudspeaker.

'Which emergency service do you require?' said a serious voice.

'And where's your father when we need him?' said Mrs Yeager in Sean's general direction.

Sean growled at this slight on his father's character. He was about to protest when the operator replied.

'I'm sorry, what did you say?'

'Oh, err, Police.'

****

Agent Lee jumped out of her chair like someone had poked her with a cattle prod. She roused a yawning colleague and addressed him in her bossiest tone.

'Wake up! There's been a security breach. This is no time for dosing!'

'Yeah, sure. I'm on it.'

Her colleague squinted and stabbed commands into a keyboard.

'Alert! Code-ten! Alert! Code-ten!' flashed a message on a bank of computer screens in front of them. Speakers repeated the words in unison. Communicators buzzed and beeped on the wrists and in the pockets of every Foundation agent in the building. Commandos ran around brandishing weapons and looking for locations to guard. It was the first time in years a security alert had been set off. In every room and corridor of the Foundation's Headquarters, people looked at each other, unsure what to do next or what *code-ten* actually meant.

'This is Brigadier Cuthbertson. Where is this *code-ten*, Control?'

'We've had a break-in at the home of a priority-one subject, sir.'

'Who is it?'

'Sean Yeager, sir,' said Lee, shaking.

'Who's that?' said Cuthbertson. 'I've never heard of him. This had better be a false alarm, or heads will roll.'

Agent Lee broke out in a cold sweat. It was unlike the Brigadier to take an interest in security or any other details for that matter.

'It looks like intruders cut a hole through an upstairs wall, sir.'

Or, to be more precise, they had removed a perfect circle from the upper side-wall of an ordinary house in broad daylight. Why on her shift? And what on Earth had they used to cut such a large hole undetected?

'I want live pictures! And get our nearest team over there on the double! I want the area secured, do you hear me?'

'I would, sir, but our spy-bots are not responding. I've used a satellite to zoom in on the house.'

'Then patch those pictures through to me! I want a full report in the next hour,' said Cuthbertson.

'I'll order a lock-down right away, sir.'

Lee tried to remember the Yeager family and shook her head. It mattered little, duty called. She sighed, relieved it would be someone else's mess to sort out, not to mention the paperwork. The Foundation didn't tolerate failure, ever. Not since the St Jacobs incident, which no one dared to discuss, in case they were somehow blamed. According to the rumour mill, it had resulted in a volcanic eruption and the destruction of half an island.

'Where is this *Sean Yeager*?' said Cuthbertson.

'We think he went shopping, sir.'

There was a long pause.

'Oops,' she thought. 'Wrong answer.'

'We think? We *think*? Someone had better know! A priority-one subject is meant to be under twenty-four-hour protection. Collect all our video and tracking data for the last forty-eight hours. I want to know *exactly* how a burglar broke into a protected house on *your* watch.'

'Yes, sir. Right away, sir.'

Lee felt her cheeks flush. She returned to her chair and summoned a colleague. Now she understood why Cuthbertson was nicknamed *the old battle-axe*. He had a point though, to be fair. Priority-one subjects were meant to be under constant guard. And how *did* someone dissolve half a wall without setting off any alarms? The Foundation had video cameras, tremor detectors, and spy-bots crawling all over the site.

Her second-in-command perched himself beside her.

'Call Surveillance. We need all their data on the Yeager house for the past two days.'

'Right away, ma'am.'

Lee winced at the prospect of sifting through hours and hours of video footage.

****

About six miles from the Yeager house, two Foundation agents sat in a booth at an old-fashioned diner. Clavity was a thickset man with a big appetite. He had waited for his club sandwich and onion rings for literally minutes. It had been an early start, and his empty stomach demanded food. The very second his order arrived, Clavity grabbed it in two shovel-sized hands and took the largest bite he could manage.

His partner, Agent Rusham, sipped mineral water and eyed him with a look of disdain. She smoothed a lock of jet-black hair behind one ear and made a bet with herself that Clavity would not make his sixtieth birthday. Not with all the rubbish he ate. Rusham was fond of Clavity, but would he listen to her advice about food and exercise? It was as likely as him being promoted to Sigma Force. She, on the other hand, was going all the way to the top, whatever it took.

The agents' watches came alive, beeping and buzzing in time. Clavity ignored the clamour and took another bite of his triple-decker sandwich.

'Major, we have a code-ten alert!' said Rusham, rising from

her seat. 'This is no time for gorging yourself. We need to fuse atoms and ship out!'

Clavity shrugged and took another bite. His mouth was crammed full, and he took an age to answer.

'It's probably another false alarm. Can't it wait a few minutes?'

'Shall we?' said Rusham, casting her most impatient look.

Clavity threw some money on the table and brought the rest of the sandwich with him. He caught the restaurant's door with his right boot, an inch before it flattened his nose. He grumbled about his untouched coffee and left the diner.

Rusham was already at the car, and Clavity hurried after her, splashing through the puddles. For a stocky man, Clavity could move surprisingly well when he set his mind on it. He landed sideways in the passenger seat and avoided head-butting his partner by a whisker. Rusham did not even blink. She was used to her partner's clumsiness, and his shambolic ways amused her.

'Who is this priority-one subject anyway?' said Clavity, between mouthfuls.

'Sean Yeager. And this is *serious*. The intruder could still be on the premises. Cuthbertson is having a fit.'

'Why?' said Clavity, shrugging.

'Because, Major,' said Rusham, staring into the vanity mirror. '*We* were meant to be there *all* morning!'

'Oops!'

Rusham lifted her sunglasses and stared into a retina scanner. She had deep brown eyes with a tawny green outer rim, a gift from her father's side.

'Welcome, Agent Rusham,' said a warm, female voice.

Hermes burst into life. In a whirr of turbines, Rusham reversed into the street and sped away.

Their white sports car attracted admiring glances as they cruised through a leafy suburb. Most people mistook Clavity and Rusham for wealthy property developers or city traders. It was an unusual disguise, but it seemed to work.

'HQ has intercepted an emergency call to the Police,' said

Rusham. 'They're sending over a squad car.'

'I'll stand down them down with a quick phone call,' said Clavity. 'Best if the boys in blue don't start snooping around.'

'And even better if they don't beat us to it,' said Rusham, with a wry smile.

In theory, Clavity was in charge.

'But look who's driving the hi-tech car,' thought Rusham, as she weaved through the traffic.

CHAPTER 2: WATCHING

On a distant world, a bell-like tone rang out in the sleeping quarters of Deijan Klesus.

'Bong! Urgent report for Deijan Klesus. Bong! Urgent report for Deijan Klesus.'

Klesus grumbled to himself. He never seemed to have a moment's peace since the latest campaign began.

'Go ahead, Alviqua,' he said in a resigned voice.

He dreaded receiving messages. Had another planetary system fallen? Could he spare any more valuable forces to engage the enemy? There was never any good news. If there was, he felt sure the sentient computers kept it to themselves.

A hologram appeared in the centre of his bedroom. It was a high-resolution figure of a woman wearing a blue jumpsuit.

'Sentient SB-12-59 wishes to report.'

'Yes, 12-59, what is it?' said Klesus, reaching for an inhaler.

The war was playing havoc with his stomach.

'Ulcers,' his robo-doctor said. 'Take some rest,' it said.

'You try running a pan-galactic war and taking a holiday,' was his usual reply.

The hologram displayed a simulated face for his benefit and its own amusement. The face smiled in a slightly spooky manner, which lacked sincerity.

'Greetings, Deijan. We have important news.'

Klesus shrugged. Wasn't it always important? Why else would the sentients disturb him when he was trying to sleep? They were always awake, always processing. He was sure they never once considered his health.

'Yes, 12-59. What is your *news*?'

'We have found what you were looking for, Deijan. On Terra Prime.'

Klesus sucked on a tube of medicine and let anti-stress vapour soothe his lungs. Great, another cryptic message.

They were his favourite, especially when he was trembling with fatigue. He tried to remember any missions he had sent to Terra Prime. Blank. Nada. Nothing. It was a young planet of no strategic importance. For a start, it was light-years from anywhere.

'What have you found, 12-59? And please keep it brief.'

Klesus knew a spy-bot was unlikely to hurry a message across several hundred light-years of folded space-time. He would be lucky to have any rest for hours, let alone the deep sleep he craved.

'We have found anomalies,' said 12-59.

'What does that mean? Explain yourself!'

This exchange could go on all night. An anomaly might be a meteorite strike, a change in the weather, or a new form of life. It could be almost anything.

'Technical and biological anomalies,' said 12-59.

Klesus felt a jolt in his heart. This was a surprise. Terra Prime was a backward planet in dire need of an idea to call its own. Next, the spy-bot would be claiming the Terrans had invented a miracle weapon. Perhaps they had developed a vaccine to wipe out the Vuloz? Now that *would* be something.

'More likely, the Vuloz have landed and enslaved every one of them,' he mused.

'We request a mind upload for evaluation,' said 12-59.

Klesus hated mind uploads. The sentients loved to beam millions of details straight into his brain. Sure, it was efficient, but afterwards the insides of his skull felt like they had been pummelled in a barbaric contact sport. Evaluation? Decision-making would be more accurate. Sentient computers were capable of gathering enough information to fill a gas giant, but could they decide on a course of action? Nope. With them, it was either verify information or launch an all-out attack, which is why the sentients had been relieved of command many years ago. And not before time. You need a strategy to defeat an enemy as cunning and adaptable as the Vuloz, or you lose. And for centuries now, the Aenaids *had* been losing despite the sentients. What Klesus needed more than anything was a fresh approach to outwit the Aenaid's mortal enemy.

'Confirm you have reliable information,' he said, staggering to the living area.

'We have verified our data with many sources, including carbon and silica-based life forms,' said 12-59.

Which meant 12-59 had been up to the spy-bots' usual trick of mind-probing life forms and breaking into primitive computer systems. It was considered unethical if you asked the legal-bots. However, in times of war, the Pentarchy considered it a necessary evil. Besides, the Terrans would not even know it had happened.

'And why should I care about these anomalies?'

Klesus realised that even the most advanced sentient would struggle to answer this question. 12-59 was probably hundreds of years old already and obsolete by modern standards. There was a long pause. Klesus reached for a chemo-patch to treat his inevitable headache.

'Might as well make this painless,' he thought.

'We believe we have found traces of the Eternal Promise,' said 12-59, in a steady tone. 'With a probability of 92%.'

Klesus fell into a reclining chair and clutched at his chest. A sharp pain spread under his ribs. However, the sentients would not let him die no matter how hard his body tried to give in. Klesus was now more than three thousand years old and kept alive against his wishes.

'The missing *scout ship*?' he said.

At last, a chance to locate Vrass, the rebel Vuloz leader, and end this infernal war. A chance to restore the Aenaid race to their rightful place and finally get some sleep.'

Klesus slumped back while nanobots worked their magic and repaired his heart from the inside. The moment he was revived, images and voices flashed into his mind. It was like watching an old-fashioned movie with the ability to steer the camera and ask questions. Except in this film, Klesus felt a steady throbbing on the inside of his skull. His cortex upgrade was long overdue, as was his re-cloning.

'Terra Prime is a water-based planet known to the resident humanoids as Earth,' said the upload.

'Yes, I *know*. What's new?'

It was about time the sentients credited him with *some* intelligence, after all the data chips they had planted in his brain over the centuries.

'Show me these anomalies,' said Klesus, closing his eyes.

Pictures and voices flooded his mind.

'By Ze'us, can you get to the point?' he said, shuddering at the thought of witnessing every detail of 12-59's report in four dimensions.

CHAPTER 3: SCRAMBLE

'Agent Clavity, this is Cuthbertson. Are you at the Yeagers' house yet?'

Cuthbertson sounded angry, perhaps he already knew about their unscheduled break for food? Clavity gestured to Rusham, who shrugged her shoulders and carried on driving. They reached a queue of traffic and slowed to a halt.

'How long until we get there?'

'In this traffic, about twenty minutes,' said Rusham, checking Hermes' touchscreen.

'We'll be there soon, sir,' said Clavity.

'I don't call twenty minutes soon, Major. Make it five, or I'll have you demoted! Over and out.'

'Gee, thanks.'

'What did you expect?' said Rusham. 'We were meant to be within two hundred yards of their house.'

Clavity glared at the back of a dirty goods lorry. It moved in fits and starts and towered above them.

'Can we take the scenic route?'

'I thought you'd never ask,' said Rusham. 'Hermes, switch to flight mode and hover at ten feet.'

There was a loud whirr, followed by a roar from the rear of the car. Parts slid and clunked into position, and they began to rise.

'Camouflage on. Hover-mode on,' said Hermes, in a calm female voice.

'Err, hang on a minute...' said Clavity, but before he had the chance to finish his sentence, they had turned sharply to the left and were hovering over a hedge.

Clavity knocked his head against the passenger window and let out a groan.

'You could have warned me!'

'I'm simply following your orders, Major. According to Hermes, we'll be at the Yeagers' house in three minutes, thirty seconds.'

'Great,' said Clavity, rubbing his ear.

They sped away and left behind a chaotic scene.

'Screech!'

The driver who witnessed Hermes' vanishing act braked to a stop.

'Crump!'

His car was rammed from behind by a white van.

'Doof!'

A large and expensive four-wheel drive piled into the white van.

'Smash! Crash! Crunch!'

A long line of vehicles slammed into the back of each other and threw shards of coloured plastic and broken headlights all over the road. A chorus of car horns sounded, and the drivers found themselves wedged into their seats by their vehicles' airbags.

Unaware of the carnage, Rusham flew Hermes at high-speed over grassy fields. She dodged the treetops and accelerated over rolling hills.

'Whoa!' said Clavity, as a herd of cows stampeded, and they skimmed the top of some trees. 'Do we *have* to fly so low?'

'It's normal procedure, said Rusham. 'We don't want to be spotted, now do we?'

Clavity sighed. He had studied the satellite pictures, and the break-in at the Yeagers was no ordinary burglary. If the thieves could cut a huge hole in a wall, what could they do to Hermes?

'Right, let's agree on a plan. First, we need to secure the house. Then we'll call in the clean-up squad. Our spy-bots aren't responding, so we need to be careful. Any questions?'

'Are we going in undercover?' said Rusham.

'Obviously! The thieves could still be inside the house. We'll use our stealth gear. I'll smooth things over with old battle-axe afterwards.'

Rusham raised her eyebrows and whistled.

'Good luck with that one.'

The countryside gave way to scattered buildings, and Hermes reached the outskirts of a town.

'We're nearly there,' said Rusham, checking a map on the console. 'Where do you want to land?'

'First, let's scan the house on infrared. If there's space, we can land further up the road.'

While they hovered, the console showed a grey image of the Yeagers' house. Inside, were two white shapes. Rusham circled back to the road and flew over a row of identical red brick houses.

'There are two life signs inside the house but no one else on the premises.'

'Prepare for landing,' said Rusham.

Hermes threw down a torrent of hot air and descended vertically into an empty parking space. It almost flattened a black cat that was rolling on its back. Fortunately, Hermes' down-draught was so fierce it blew the feline sideways into a front garden. The cat righted itself and staggered away in a daze.

'Major, your orders are to secure the area and no heroics, do you hear me?' said Cuthbertson.

'Yes, sir,' said Clavity.

Clavity and Rusham opened a floor locker inside Hermes and selected an array of gear. In the confined space, they twisted and contorted to pull on their stealth suits.

'Set your blaster to stun,' said Clavity. 'Ready?'

Rusham gave a thumbs-up.

Rusham and Clavity exited Hermes and appeared out of nowhere, in a quiet, residential road. A young mother approached, pushing a baby buggy. She broke into a trot and hurried past them, shaking her head. Meanwhile, Hermes sealed its doors and blended into the background.

Clavity and Rusham took opposite sides of the road and stalked towards the Yeager house. Hidden from the naked eye, they reflected a blurred image of the scenery around them. Clavity watched Rusham through his visor. She knelt, pulled a device from her suit, and swept it in the air before studying its read-out.

'Anything on the scanner?' said Clavity.

'Nothing much, but I'm picking up a strange background reading.'

'Alright, I'm going in. Cover me.'

'Yes, sir!'

Clavity ran towards the Yeagers' house. He bounded across their front lawn and took off. With his hover-pack on full power, he climbed up the front of the house and soared over its roof. There was a crackle on his communicator.

'What in blazes are you doing, Clavity?' said Cuthbertson.

'Securing the area, sir.'

Clavity hovered above a chimney and swept the garden with his scanner.

'Clear on UV, infrared, and radar. If anyone's hiding down there, they have better gear than us.'

He turned his attention to the side of the house. It was an ordinary dwelling with a large, oval hole where its bedroom wall should have been.

'I'm surprised the roof hasn't caved in,' said Clavity.

He hovered down the side of the house and peered into the exposed bedroom. A boy wearing a bright blue t-shirt stood behind a bed and waved at him. Clavity's communicator fell silent. He flew around the house and landed near the front door.

'How did that boy see me? I'm invisible!'

Rusham arrived and gave Clavity a nudge on the arm.

'Having fun?'

'What's your status, Major?' said Cuthbertson in a haughty tone.

Clavity turned to Rusham.

'All clear?'

'Yes, sir. And totally invisible,' said Rusham.

'We're ready for the clean-up squad, sir.'

'Shame about your power pack,' whispered Rusham. 'I expect the neighbours will be phoning the Police anytime now.'

Clavity gulped.

Further down the road, two men waited in a battered red van. They watched Clavity on a screen and steered a camera drone using a tiny joystick.

'You see that, Greerbo? You see what we're up against?' said a thin, bearded man with penetrating eyes. 'I told you we were too slow!'

'Yes, boss. I mean, no, boss. Shall we leave now, boss?'

Greerbo was a short, stocky man with an ugly face. His twisted nose, the result of one too many brawls.

'Not yet, we don't want to attract attention, do we?' said Krankhausen.

The men continued to watch Clavity. After a few minutes, Greerbo could hold his tongue no longer.

'I still don't get it, boss. If the kid's so important, why don't we kidnap him? It would be much easier.'

Krankhausen looked as though he might explode with rage. Instead, a cruel smile stretched his face.

'Greerbo, are you questioning my judgement?'

'Err, no, boss. I was just wondering.'

'You see those piles of junk?' said Krankhausen, gesturing to three crates on the floor behind them.

'Yes, boss?'

'They don't need feeding, they won't scream, and most importantly, they won't try and escape.'

Krankhausen reached into one and pulled out a thin brown hair.

'*This* is our prize, Greerbo. All we need are a few strands of the Yeager brat's DNA, and Deveraux will pay us a fortune.'

'Why's that, boss?'

'So he can clone him, Greerbo.'

'A kid?'

Krankhausen sighed.

'Don't worry about it. It's way above your pay grade.'

21

CHAPTER 4: INVESTIGATION

The Yeagers' front door swung open.

'That's him!' said Sean, pointing at Clavity.

'What are you playing at, clambering all over my roof?' said Mrs Yeager.

'Err, Police, ma'am,' said Clavity, taking off his helmet. 'We're investigating a break-in.'

'Police, huh?' said Mrs Yeager. 'Can I see your badge?'

Clavity fumbled in his pocket and produced a black wallet containing a gold shield. Beneath the shield, a green light flashed in a rhythmic pattern.

'Do I look like an idiot?' said Mrs Yeager.

Clavity frowned. The hypnotic circuits in Foundation identity badges were potent enough to convince most people Clavity was a tap-dancing mouse if necessary.

'I mean, do the Police carry MPA280 blasters?' she said, pointing at the weapon at Clavity's hip. 'And by the way, those hypnotic badges have never worked on me.'

Clavity winced and Rusham, still hidden by her camouflage, chuckled beside him.

'And do the Police wear anti-gravity hover-packs with light field reflector plates, and I'm guessing…a flat battery pack?'

'I, uh…'

Clavity cleared his throat to explain, but words failed him. This time he was well and truly busted. He noticed Sean staring at him and felt like an exhibit in a museum.

'Is your camera on?' said Mrs Yeager, waving her hand in front of Clavity's visor. 'Brigadier, can you call off the goon squad and send builders over to repair my house?'

Clavity's mobile phone rang. He answered and handed it to Mrs Yeager.

'The Brigadier would like a word, ma'am.'

'Ah, Brigadier, good to hear from you. If I remember correctly, you promised I would never see your little helpers ever again?'

'I'm sorry, Mrs Yeager. But we still need to keep an eye on you.'

'And a great job you're doing. Where exactly *is* the rest of my house?'

'Hmm, I can understand you're a little upset...'

'And what about my husband? Have you managed to find him yet?'

'Err, not as such. Look, Mrs Yeager, if we can take a look around, I'm sure we can come to some arrangement.'

Mrs Yeager sighed. What choice did she have? If she allowed the Foundation back into her life, she would probably find them nosing around her garden in the middle of the night. On the other hand, what about the bedroom wall?

'Alright, I'll agree on one condition – that you repair my house *today*.'

Mrs Yeager shook her head in disbelief. For all she knew, it was the Foundation who had melted her wall in the first place. But why? Then again, what was one of their goons doing climbing all over her roof?

'Agreed,' said Cuthbertson. 'Can you pass me back to Major Clavity?'

Mrs Yeager handed Clavity the phone and gave him a withering look. He gave a sheepish nod.

'Yes, Brigadier. Loud and clear. We'll secure the area right away.'

As he spoke, a small blue car pulled into an empty parking space further along the road.

'Crunch!'

Its bonnet crumpled like tin foil and caved in on itself. The car rolled backwards, and radiator fluid gushed onto the road. The vehicle came to a halt, and its front grill clattered on the tarmac. Clavity let out a groan. Hermes flickered into sight and wailed a siren at the offending driver. Its bodywork was gleaming and unmarked.

'Rusham, can you go and sort things out?' said Clavity.

Agent Rusham appeared beside him, to the surprise of the Yeagers.

'Yes, I'd love to,' she said sarcastically. 'Is there anything else you'd like me to clear up, your highness?'

Clavity gave her a harsh stare, and Rusham shook her head. She strutted across the road in a huff. Halfway across, she stopped and hurried back to the house, brandishing the scanner.

'Now what?' said Clavity.

'Ionic radiation,' said Rusham. 'And it's nearby.'

As she spoke, a red van crawled past, and the scanner beeped even louder.

'Fetch Hermes,' said Clavity.

Rusham gave him a dirty look.

'And what about Cuthbertson?'

'We'll explain everything later.'

'On your head be it,' said Rusham, sprinting across the road.

Keen to see what was going on, Sean wandered after her. Halfway across the road, his attention was drawn by a howling noise from the red van. Its wheels smoked wildly, and it accelerated towards him like a dragster.

'Watch out!' cried Clavity, diving to pull Sean away.

Sean rolled to one side, and the van sped past, missing him by a hair's breadth. He watched in disbelief as it raced away.

'What a maniac!' he cried.

Clavity pulled out a sidearm and took aim.

'Better not,' he thought. Today had been bad enough already without risking the neighbourhood. His knowledge on the subject was shaky, but Clavity was pretty sure a blaster round and ionic radiation would cause an explosion.

The van skidded around the stricken, blue car and howled away down the road.

'That was close,' said Clavity, offering Sean a hand.

Before Sean could reply, Hermes arrived and almost ran over Clavity.

'Hey!' he cried, leaping out of the way.

A passenger door rose like a wing.

'Come on then!' said Rusham. 'They're getting away!'

Clavity helped Sean to his feet.

'I'll be right there.'

Sean considered his options. He could stay at home and let the thieves get away, or go after them in a high-tech car? It was not a difficult decision.

'Were they the intruders?' said Clavity.

Rusham gave a shrug.

'There's only one way to find out.'

Before Clavity could decide, Sean dived into Hermes and occupied the passenger seat.

'Hey! What do you think you're doing?' said Rusham.

'What are we waiting for?' said Sean. 'Let's get them!'

Clavity groaned and clambered into the back.

'At least this way, we can make sure he's safe?'

Rusham shook her head.

'I don't want to be in your shoes when Cuthbertson finds out.'

Mrs Yeager sprinted down the pavement towards them.

'Sean Yeager! Come back here this instant!'

Sean could just make out his mother's voice, but her words were lost in the roar of Hermes' engine as it screeched away. Mrs Yeager stood and screamed at the departing car.

An elderly gentleman staggered towards her. His face was ghostly white, and a trickle of blood dribbled down his cheek.

'Someone drove into my car. Did you see where they went?'

Mrs Yeager sighed.

'Come in and have a cup of tea, Mr Shawcross. And let's have a look at your cut.'

Mrs Yeager cursed under her breath and prayed Sean would be safe. She vowed to give Cuthbertson a stern talking to when she finally found her phone.

****

'Clavity, what's going on?'

It was Cuthbertson. By now, he was probably having his third kitten. Clavity adjusted his earpiece.

'We're heading east in pursuit of a suspect. Agent Rusham detected an ionic drive.'

'Major, I told you to protect the Yeagers!'

'Oh, Sean Yeager is right here with us now, sir.'

There was an audible gasp.

'You've taken him *with* you? And what about Mrs Yeager?'

'I believe she's talking to the clean-up squad, sir.'

'Who's that?' said Sean.

'Our boss,' whispered Rusham, putting a finger to her lips.

Rusham turned onto a busy road in pursuit of the red van. It sped away, and its sides folded outwards into triangular wings. Moments later, its rear doors parted to reveal three cone-shaped exhausts. In a sudden burst of flames, the van rose into the sky and was gone. It left in its wake, a family car with smoke pouring from its paintwork.

'Watch out!' cried Clavity.

'I'm on it,' said Rusham, steering around the burning vehicle. She turned off the main road.

Cuthbertson continued on Hermes' intercom.

'Major, do I have to tell you how many regulations…blah, blah, blah, blah, blah…'

But Clavity was preoccupied with Hermes' scanner.

'We are tracking a flying van, accelerating away from our position and heading due south. Permission to pursue, sir?'

'Flying van?' said Cuthbertson. 'Control, do you have anything on your radar?'

There was a pause and some muffled voices at HQ.

'Vanished? Where?' said Cuthbertson. 'Okay, Clavity, follow them but do not engage. Repeat, do not engage. Do you hear me?'

'Will do, sir,' said Clavity, leaning between the front seats. 'You heard the man, Rusham. Do you have their heading?'

'I'm on it,' she said, tapping the console.

Rusham steered Hermes into a quiet, residential road lined

with cherry trees.

'Belts on everyone.'

Sean pulled a Y-shaped harness over his shoulders and clicked it into a circular clasp.

'Cool! Wait until my friends hear about this.'

'Best keep this yourself, Sean,' said Clavity. 'We'll talk about it later. Okay, Rusham, you know what to do.'

She busied herself at the controls.

'Hermes, engage camouflage. Switch to flight mode and hover at thirty feet.'

'Flight mode confirmed,' said a calm female voice.

Motors whirred, and wing pieces slid into position as Hermes climbed above the trees. Sean watched stabiliser fins extend from the front of the car and heard the wheel arches seal.

'What does this button do?' he said, eyeing a bright red control on the dashboard.

'Keep your hands away!' said Rusham.

Intrigued by its texture, Sean trailed his finger a fraction above the glowing, red button. There was a loud roar, and he was thrown back in his seat.

'Ahhh!'

Sean's cheeks quivered like jellies, and his neck strained with acceleration. Clavity was thrown across the rear seat, his seatbelt flapping.

'Sorry,' said Sean.

Rusham regained control and wiped her brow. She gave a nervous smile.

'Right, we're still alive. Master Yeager, I need you to keep your hands in your pockets. Do *not* touch anything. Do you understand?'

Shaken, Sean gave a silent nod.

'I'm alright. Don't worry about me,' said Clavity behind them.

Rusham rolled her eyes.

'Hermes, switch to ionic scan and track the course of a target heading south.'

'Ionic scan active,' said Hermes.

A colourful map appeared on the inside of the windscreen. It showed a green trail stretching over rolling contours of land and coastline. The target was now a distant, orange spec near the edge of the windscreen.

'Ouch! I've hurt my neck,' said Clavity.

'Having a good flight, Major?' said Rusham.

'Wonderful. Any sign of the van?

'We're on its trail.'

'And it's escaping!' said Sean.

'Not for long,' said Rusham.

Cuthbertson's voice returned on the intercom.

'Clavity, what in blazes are you doing? I've had the Fire Brigade on the phone complaining about some trees you roasted!'

Sean blushed and gazed at the landscape below. He could sense Rusham glowering in his direction.

CHAPTER 5: PURSUIT

Hermes' instrument panel flickered.

'Where's the target gone?' said Clavity.

'They're fifty miles away and increasing,' said Rusham. 'If we don't do something, we're going to lose them.'

'How much fuel do we have left?'

'Enough,' said Rusham. 'Do you want to risk it?'

Clavity considered the situation. If the van escaped, so did their best chance of catching the intruder. Or was it a coincidence that a sky-van powered by an ionic drive had left the Yeagers' house in a hurry?

'Fuse some atoms!' said Clavity. 'We can't let them get away.'

'Brace yourselves,' said Rusham. 'Engaging particle-drive in three, two, one.'

Hermes shuddered as they picked up speed, and Sean felt his stomach tighten.

'This is better than a roller coaster!'

'It sure is,' said Rusham, grinning.

In a few minutes, the van became a steady blip in the middle of the windscreen. Sean stared outside and noticed a distant dot cruising below the clouds.

'We have visual contact, Major,' said Rusham.

'Have you gone completely mad?' said Cuthbertson. 'Half the country's reported a sonic boom, and I've had the Air Force on the phone telling me they've launched fighters to intercept you!'

'We're pursuing the van, sir,' said Rusham.

'Did it occur to you to engage stealth mode, Agent Rusham? Or have you broken that as well?'

'Yes, sir.'

'It occurred to you, or you've broken it?' said Cuthbertson.

'Both, sir,' said Rusham. 'Major?'

Clavity leaned forwards and whispered.

'Tell him we're in hot pursuit of the intruder.'

'You're lighting up our tracking screen like a rash on a baby's bottom,' said Cuthbertson.

'Missile alert! Missile alert! Range three thousand metres and closing,' said Hermes, in her usual calm voice.

'Take evasive action!' said Clavity, hurrying to strap himself in.

Rusham threw Hermes sideways and upwards into a vertical climb.

'Missile lock! Missile lock!'

'Hermes, deploy counter-measures,' said Rusham.

There was a burst on either side of the vehicle, and Hermes threw out debris. Rusham gained height and steered into a right turn, followed by a steep dive. Sean watched a patchwork of green become fields and hedges at an alarming rate. His weight hung forwards, held in place by the harness.

'I think I'm going to be sick.'

'Save it for later,' said Rusham.

Hermes instrument panel lit up.

'Ground warning! Ground warning!'

At the last second, Rusham pulled out of their dive and banked hard to the left.

'Boom!' 'Boom!'

Missiles exploded above the ground, and Hermes rocked with the shockwave.

'Phew! That was close,' said Rusham, levelling out.

'Great job!' said Clavity. 'Can we still track the van?'

'Sure can,' said Rusham, accelerating once more.

A new voice crackled on the intercom.

'Enjoying your ride, you bumbling idiots? Follow me if you dare!'

The speaker clicked and fell silent.

'Who in tarnation is that?' said Clavity.

'Our missile-wielding friend, I expect,' said Rusham. 'Something's blocking our communications channel. We're on our own, Major.'

'I think he's called Krank..hausen,' said Sean. In his mind, he pictured a bearded face and penetrating eyes. He felt a queasy shudder ripple through his body.

'Von Krankhausen?' said Clavity. 'I thought we caught that old goat years ago?'

'We did, but he escaped. No one's seen him for years, said Rusham. 'How do you know about him, Sean?'

'It just came to me,' said Sean, staring out of the side window.

'Hermes, run a voice match on the target's message,' said Rusham.

'Affirmative.'

Sean watched the blip move closer. Beneath them, land gave way to grey water and tiny flecks of white.

'The target's voice matches Egbert Von Krankhausen, visual on screen now,' said Hermes.

Sean trembled as a cruel face appeared on the console. It was a middle-aged man with dark hair and a pointed goatee. He held a black and white numbered board in front of his chest.

'Do you recognise him, Sean?' said Rusham.

The face had the same cold eyes and pallid skin, but the man's hair seemed longer and darker than Sean imagined.

'Sort of, but his hair looks different.'

'Radar lock! Radar lock!'

'Here we go again,' said Clavity.

'Not so fast, Krankhausen,' said Rusham. 'Hermes, engage lasers, full power.'

'Confirmed,' said the calm voice.

'You heard Cuthbertson. We can't shoot him down,' said Clavity.

'Yeah? Well, I'm not going to be shot down either,' said Rusham.

Clavity tried to reach between the seats but was unable to move because of his harness. The tracking display flashed and went blank.

'Now where's he gone?'

'Hermes, show the target's last position,' said Rusham.

33

'On screen now.'

'They can't be,' said Clavity. 'That's underground!'

'Not underground, Major. Underwater!'

Rusham put Hermes into a shallow dive and reduced their speed. She slowed until they were hovering just above the water.

'Switch to underwater mode,' said Rusham. 'Hold tight, everyone! Here we go!'

Hermes skimmed the waves, and hydraulic motors adjusted its control surfaces. A few seconds later, they tipped head-first into the sea with a giant splash. When the bubbles had cleared, a gentle sound of motors hummed behind them. Outside, there was nothing but a dark blue fog of seawater.

'No sign of the target on sonar,' said Rusham.

'Do we have a thermal trace?' said Clavity.

'No, the seawater's too dense. Any ideas?'

'Enjoying your swim?' said a familiar voice. 'Adieu, Foundation fools!'

Sean and Rusham glanced at each other.

'I have a bad feeling about this,' said Sean.

'What do you mean?' said Rusham.

Before Sean could reply, a sonar pip echoed around them. It bounced against Hermes and reflected away into the ocean. Moments later, there was a deep thud, and the lights went out. They found themselves sitting in darkness with only the creaks and groans of Hermes' hull for company.

'The controls have gone dead!' said Rusham.

A faint, red lamp came on and yielded barely enough light to see. The console was blank, and the fan motors were silent.

'Hermes?' said Rusham, 'Hermes?'

Her question hung in the air unanswered.

They began to drift and sank further into the gloomy depths.

'We can't just sit here,' said Sean.

Rusham woke from her daze.

'Prepare for emergency flotation. In three, two, one.'

Rusham opened a cover beneath the steering column and

flicked a switch. After a short delay, bubbles rushed from pods on either side of Hermes' hull, and they jerked upwards.

'I hope this works,' said Clavity.

Hermes broke through the surface and bounced. Large, white floats encircled the vehicle, and it began to rise and fall on the waves. Sean let out a sigh as warm, yellow sunlight filled the car. For a few minutes, no one spoke.

'Ye gads, what's that?' said Clavity.

To their left, a large, blue and white shape loomed above the sea. Several stories tall, it was heading towards them on a collision course.

'It's a ship! Dive! Dive!' said Clavity.

'We can't, Major. We don't have any power.'

The ship continued on its course and sounded a deep horn.

'It's a ferry,' said Sean.

'And ferries don't change course for anyone,' said Clavity. 'How do we open the roof?'

'We can't. The hull's pressurised. All we can do is blast our way out, which would probably sink us. Besides, what are we going to do, swim?'

Clavity felt for catches on the ceiling.

'There must be a way out?'

'Can't we just open the windows?' said Sean.

Sunlight gave way to shadows. Soon, they were enclosed on two sides by the enormous hulls of a catamaran ferry. There was an approaching rumble of powerful engines, and Hermes scraped against one of the ferry's hulls. One of its floats burst.

'What was that?' said Clavity.

However, there was no reply. The roar of the ferry's engines drowned out all attempts of conversation. Hermes was dragged backwards by a powerful undercurrent. It clipped something near the ferry's stern and was pulled under. After two of the longest minutes Sean had ever known, Hermes bounced back to the surface and dipped to one side in the ferry's wake.

No one dared to speak until the engine noise had faded. Hermes sagged towards the rear, and the three passengers slumped in their seats, exhausted but glad to be alive. Sean gazed at the sky and felt Hermes bob up and down. He spotted a dark, triangular shape cutting through the water. It turned and vanished beneath the surface.

'Uh oh! There's a shark out there.'

'A shark? Where?' said Rusham, leaning across his seat to take a look.

'I think it went underneath us.'

There was a sharp bump on the underside of the stricken vehicle.

'Woah!' said Clavity.

Sean held his breath and waited for another impact. Instead, a phone buzzed and vibrated on the back seat.

'Clavity here. Yes, sir. Our mission status?'

Rusham gave a deep sigh and arched her eyebrows.

'We're adrift at sea, being prodded by sharks. No, Krankhausen's got away.'

There were muffled sounds of an angry voice.

'Yes, sir, I realise it's not a fishing trip. Of course, sir.'

Clavity gave a harried look.

'Yes, sir, I believe our beacon is working. No, we're not going anywhere.'

'Unless the sharks eat us,' said Sean.

His words broke the tension, and Rusham chuckled. Clavity joined in, and soon all three of them were laughing. Clavity dropped the phone on the seat, and it switched to speaker mode.

'What did you say? Why are you laughing? I fail to see what's so amusing about your predicament. Blah, blah, blah-blah, blah.'

But no one was listening. Clavity ended the call.

'HQ? Who needs 'em, eh?'

'Err, we do, Major,' said Rusham. 'My feet are getting wet.'

CHAPTER 6: DISCOVERY

Agent Lee climbed out of a battered transit van. To the casual passer-by, it was a wreck. However, it was packed with hi-tech equipment. Lee was unused to field operations and missed the comfort of her chair and coffee machine. Still, it was not all bad - at least she could breathe some fresh air and maybe shed a few pounds. Cuthbertson was adamant, he wanted answers about the break-in, and he wanted them right away. Unfortunately, the video footage they had recovered from the Yeagers' house was blank. It had either been disabled, or someone had blocked the camera's transmissions.

'Right, team, let's get to it. You know the drill. Cuthbertson wants a report in the next two hours.'

The team hurried into action. The Foundation was under attack for the first time in a decade, and they needed clues fast.

'Hey, get off my flowerbed!' said Mrs Yeager to a man in blue overalls. She stood on the front doorstep in her flip-flops with a look of disgust on her face.

'We're from the Gas Board. Someone's reported a leak.'

'Really? Then perhaps you can explain how the gas pipe moved from over there?' said Mrs Yeager, pointing at an exposed, grey pipe jutting out of the garage wall.

'I, err.'

Lee overheard the conversation and came to the aid of her colleague.

'Mrs Yeager, my name is Alison Lee. We're investigating the burglary. Perhaps Brigadier Cuthbertson briefed you?'

Mrs Yeager studied Lee and her badge before smiling.

'Alison, do you have a phone?' she said politely.

'Err, yes.'

'Can you do me a *big* favour and call Brigadier Cuthbertson? I'd like a quick chat.'

'Uh, yes, of course.'

Lee speed dialled and handed the phone to Mrs Yeager. It rang for a few moments.

'Agent Lee? About time! What have you discovered?'

'Gas pipes and a very angry mother!' said Mrs Yeager.

'Err, what?' said Cuthbertson.

'What have you done with my son?'

Lee paled and tried to recover the phone, but Mrs Yeager turned her body.

'Err, who *is* this?'

'The least you could have done is call me!'

'Mrs Yeager? Your uh, son is quite safe. We'll have him home in no time.'

Lee was worried now and called to her team. Quick as a flash, three figures in blue suits surrounded Mrs Yeager. Two seized her arms, and the other touched a device against her neck.

'I've been worried sick! Your minions drove off without so much as a…'

In mid-sentence, Mrs Yeager slumped into the agents' arms.

'Take her inside and keep a close eye on her,' said Lee, retrieving the phone.

'Brigadier? Yes, we have everything under control. Can Professor Quark come on-site? We have some unusual readings.'

The roof creaked behind her, and a handful of tiles smashed on the ground. A deep crack appeared above the now-infamous hole.

'And we're going to need a team of engineers to prop up the Yeagers' house.'

****

'Captain Reynard, come in and take a seat. I have a little job for you,' said Cuthbertson.

'Yes, sir. How can I help?'

Reynard was fit and muscular. He wore short-cropped

dark hair and a blue and grey camouflaged uniform complete with a sidearm. Reynard folded his cap between two large hands and sat in a leather armchair facing Cuthbertson's desk.

'First, I need a recovery team to rescue our *elite* agents,' said Cuthbertson. 'They are currently adrift here, in the middle of the Channel. I need them, and whatever's left of their vehicle, returned to HQ.'

'No problem, sir, I have a recovery team on their way,' said Reynard. 'I'm confident we'll reach them within the hour.'

'Excellent,' said Cuthbertson. 'We also need to stop Von Krankhausen once and for all. We believe he has a new sponsor, and Krankhausen is a threat to our entire operation.'

Reynard nodded gravely.

'I heard he was an ageing has-been, sir?'

'Captain, Von Krankhausen is a mercenary industrialist, and he's dangerous. He escaped from prison last year, and we need to recapture him as soon as possible. The Founder is keen to bring this matter to a rapid conclusion.'

'Understood, sir,' said Reynard. 'Sigma Force is standing by. All we need is his location.'

'Excellent. And one more thing, Captain,' said Cuthbertson, rubbing his moustache. 'Keep a close eye on Clavity and Rusham, will you? Don't let them break anything.'

'Will do, sir,' said Reynard, smiling.

After Reynard left, Cuthbertson stalked the hallway in measured strides. He felt a deep unease but was unable to establish why. He reached an elevator and punched in his passcode. Cuthbertson stared into an eye scanner and activated the elevator's controls.

'Welcome, Brigadier. Please select your floor.'

'Laboratory.'

The elevator plunged deep underground and shuddered to a halt. Two sets of doors opened, and Cuthbertson marched into a brightly lit room filled with equipment.

'Professor, may I have a word?'

An older man, wearing glasses and a bald patch, sat at a

screen studying a graph. He seemed unaware that anyone else was in the room. Around him, technicians buzzed like worker bees, too busy to greet their visitor.

'Professor?' said Cuthbertson. 'Professor!'

'No need to shout, Henry,' said Quark, adjusting his glasses. 'The readings confirm what we first thought.'

'What readings? What did we think?'

Cuthbertson often wondered if Quark lived on the same planet as everyone else. Or perhaps he was only visiting?

'There are anti-matter collision artefacts here in the upper spectrum,' said Quark. 'Which, combined with the residual neutrino traces…'

'Professor, I have no idea what you're talking about. What does all this gobbledygook mean in plain English?'

Quark paused for a moment and looked almost offended. He raised his glasses onto his forehead.

'In simple terms, Brigadier, Krankhausen used a Matteract to melt the Yeagers' wall.'

'But…' said Cuthbertson before he was interrupted.

'Yes, he most likely stole it from the Foundation. Which means we also have a security breach.' Quark paused. 'By the way, am I still needed at the Yeager house?'

Cuthbertson was speechless. He steadied himself on a chair.

'A mole? Here?'

Quark nodded.

'But Krankhausen could kill millions?'

'Yes, he is considered to be criminally insane.'

Cuthbertson was aghast at the news. A whole city could be wiped out in seconds. On *his* watch, with *his* weapons!

'Fortunately, creating anti-matter fuel is likely to be beyond Krankhausen's capabilities,' said Quark.

Cuthbertson raised his eyebrows.

'Why's that?'

'Because he would need a particle accelerator,' said Quark. 'And we know how long it takes to fund one of those, don't we?'

'Thank you, Professor. I need your team to be vigilant. We must find Krankhausen and this mole as soon as possible.'

'Yes, Brigadier. I have a few ideas,' said Quark, returning to his work. 'Now then,' he said, tapping at his computer.

Cuthbertson felt his legs weaken and staggered to the elevator. He returned to his office and used a bug detector to check every crevice and electrical device. Cuthbertson unplugged all his equipment, including the light fittings, and pulled the blinds shut. Safe in the knowledge no one could hear him, he rang Security on an encrypted phone. There was no reply, so he left a voicemail.

'Where in tarnation are you, Jenkins?'

****

Anxious for news about his ill-gotten acquisitions, Egbert Von Krankhausen led Greerbo to a laboratory at the heart of his base. Below him, the sea washed tirelessly against eight enormous steel legs that supported the structure and, ultimately, his plans.

'Have you finished yet?' he demanded of a figure dressed in a white lab coat. 'Make it quick. I'm a busy man.'

Greerbo stood glowering beside him and stretched his arms.

'I have extracted DNA from the hair samples you brought me,' said the technician. 'However, I've encountered a few problems.'

'Problems? I pay you to solve problems, not create them.'

Greerbo clicked his knuckles in agreement.

'You see the base pairs are not, err, normal,' said the technician.

'Make sense quickly, or I'll ask Greerbo here to teach you how to dive,' said Krankhausen.

The technician's hands started to shake, and beads of sweat appeared on his forehead.

'What I mean, sir, is that this DNA has mutated. Instead of *four* base chemicals, or nucleotides, it has at least *six*.'

Krankhausen scowled at the technician and gestured to Greerbo, who flexed his arms.

'It seems you have a new diving student, Greerbo.'

'Err, what I meant to say, is that this is not normal human DNA,' said the technician.

'Excellent,' said Krankhausen, smiling. 'Regrettably, Greerbo, your services will not be required today, after all.'

Greerbo sighed and stomped off in the direction of the gym.

'I trust you have some clean samples for me?' said Krankhausen.

The technician swallowed hard.

'I'll make a start on it right away.'

'See that you do,' said Krankhausen, staring out to sea. 'I hear it would take several weeks to swim home.'

****

Agent Lee retrieved a motionless spy-bot from a flowerbed. It was the size of her hand, and crumbs of soil clung to its outer skin. The spy-bot resembled an oversized, mechanical insect with legs, a body, and antennae. Lee checked it for signs of damage and found it was intact. In normal conditions, spy-bots could run for years on one power pack. However, for some reason, this one had seized up. She detached its outer casing and tested its energy cell. It appeared to be fully charged.

'Agent Brown, here's another one. I need you to run a full diagnostic. Let me know as soon as you have the results.'

'Yes, sir,' said Brown, taking it in both hands.

It was the fifth broken spy-bot her team had recovered from the Yeager site. They ranged from burrowers to tree climbers and camouflaged roamers. Each was in good condition, yet none of them showed any signs of life. Brown carried the spy-bot under a tunnel of blue plastic sheets to the field van.

Officially, the Yeagers' house was being investigated

following a gas explosion. However, passing neighbours decided it was the scene of a crime. And they were not far wrong.

Lee returned to the house and found Mrs Yeager still asleep on the sofa. A medic kept watch and took her pulse every half hour as a precaution. He found the situation highly irregular and expressed concern about his patient.

Engineers arrived and installed scaffolding and hydraulic jacks to prevent the Yeagers' roof from collapsing. They also covered the hole in Sean's bedroom wall with plastic sheeting. It was ugly but effective. The Yeagers' house now resembled a building site. Agent Lee made a phone call.

'Professor, I need your help. Yes, I realise you're busy. Can we at least send you our spy-bot data? No? Why's that? Communications lockdown? On whose orders? Cuthbertson's? Alright, I guess we'll bring our data back in the van. Okay, see you later. Bye.'

Lee shook her head in frustration.

'A fat lot of help you are,' she muttered on her way back to the field van.

'Why would Cuthbertson order a lock-down?' said Brown. 'Are we under attack?'

Lee shrugged.

'Beats me,' she said, keeping her suspicions to herself.

****

Egbert Von Krankhausen was in the middle of an important phone call when Greerbo knocked at his office door.

'Can't you see I'm busy?' he said, muting the line.

'It's our buyer, sir,' said Greerbo. 'He says it's urgent.'

Krankhausen's eyes lit up.

'Thank you, Greerbo. Tell him I'll be there in a moment.'

Krankhausen returned to his phone call and put on his most serious voice.

'As I was saying, either you send me the passcodes I've

requested, or you won't see your sister for a very long time. Do I make myself clear? Good.'

Krankhausen chuckled to himself as he covered the short distance from his office to the conference room.

'Greerbo, our mole needs a little more convincing. See what ideas you can come up with.'

'Yes, sir,' said Greerbo, leaving the room.

A gaunt face wearing dark glasses filled a large screen on the wall.

'About time, Krankhausen!'

'My apologies, I had an urgent matter to attend to.'

Krankhausen sat at a desk and took out a notebook. The figure on the screen grimaced.

'Look, Krankhausen, I have no intention of paying you ten million dollars in gold for some meagre DNA samples. Why should I when I've already invested billions in your operation?'

Krankhausen was taken aback for a moment. Perhaps he had misjudged the situation?

'It may interest you to know that this DNA came from a Foundation source?'

'Yes, I know, and what of it?' said the figure. 'We can kidnap a Foundation agent whenever we like.'

'But you see, this is not *from* a Foundation agent,' said Krankhausen.

'Agent, commando, cook. What difference does it make?'

The figure removed his sunglasses to reveal bloodshot eyes.

'You are trying my patience, Egbert!'

'You don't understand,' said Krankhausen. 'This sample is not human.'

'So where did it come from? A goldfish? A porcupine?'

'No, Mr Deveraux, it's from a Foundation priority-one subject. An ideal source for cloning your next generation of warriors.'

'Hmm,' said Deveraux, smirking. 'Interesting.'

Deveraux's mood darkened abruptly. He slipped the

sunglasses back on and appeared to be typing.

'Bring your samples to the coordinates I'm sending you. Be there tomorrow at twelve hundred hours sharp. And don't be late, Egbert. Otherwise, the next time we'll meet will be at your funeral.'

The screen went blank, leaving Krankhausen alone with his racing heartbeat.

'Yes, Mr Deveraux. Whatever you say.'

CHAPTER 7: CLUES

Sean and Agent Rusham took a seat in a waiting room at the Foundation's Medical Centre. They were greeted by a doctor carrying a tablet computer.

'Good news, you're in great health.'

'Phew,' said Sean.

'But I must say you have an unusual genetic profile.'

'How do you mean?'

'Oh, it's nothing to worry about,' said a tall man, who appeared beside them, as if from nowhere.

'Founder?' said Rusham, rising to salute.

'Please, call me Cassius.'

Cassius Olandis sat opposite Sean and stretched out his long legs.

'I expect you're wondering why you're here?'

'And why Krankhausen stole all my stuff?' said Sean.

'The good news is - you are *not* the chosen one,' said Olandis. 'We'll leave all those fanciful notions to the movies, shall we?'

Sean laughed.

'But you are very special to us, Sean. So please be careful.'

'I will.'

'And learn to trust your instincts. It's surprising how often they can bear fruit.'

Sean looked puzzled.

'Don't worry, we'll bring Krankhausen to heel. Good day to you, Sean. Agent Rusham, take good care of this young man.'

'Will do, sir,' said Rusham, standing to attention.

And with that, Olandis was gone, as quickly as he had appeared.

A receptionist approached.

'Your driver is waiting for you at the main reception.'

'Thanks,' said Rusham. 'Let's go, Sean. We need to get you

home.' Rusham clicked her phone. 'Major? We have the all-clear. See you downstairs.'

****

'My house is just around the corner,' said Sean, leading the way.

Clavity squelched across the road, his shoes still sopping wet. Rusham traipsed along beside him, wearing a deep frown.

'And whose idea was it to go after Krankhausen?'

'How was I to know what would happen?' said Clavity, keeping one eye on their surroundings.

Professor Quark had banned them from using Foundation vehicles until further notice. Anyone would think Hermes had been destroyed. True, it was a little seized up and full of seawater, but surely Quark's technicians could sort it out? To cap it all, their driver had refused to take them anywhere near the house in case there was another gas explosion.

Sean hurried home. He found the pavement blocked by blue and white tape. Two men wearing black uniforms stood guard. Beyond them, a tunnel of blue plastic stretched from a white van on the driveway to the front door. Sean tried to dodge under the tape.

'I need you to go around,' said one of the policemen.

The second policeman noticed Clavity and looked bashful.

'Don't worry about him, Major. He's new.'

Clavity gave a half-hearted smile and made a point of showing them his identity badge.

'Sorry, sir. Just doing my job.'

'Quite right too. This *is* a lock-down, gentlemen. And lay off the policeman shtick. We don't want to get caught, do we?'

The first guard winked.

'We'll keep it low-key, sir.'

The second guard smiled.

'How was your fishing trip, sir? I heard you caught a

shark?'

'Careful, sunny, or I'll arrange an introduction.'

The guards laughed and stood to one side.

As he passed the van, Clavity peered inside and waved at an agent. Anxious not to miss anything, Sean craned his neck around the van's open door. When he saw what was inside, his eyes nearly popped out of his head. The van was packed with tools, lights, and electronic equipment. A large, insect-like creature scuttled across the floor towards him. It had the appearance of a giant, mechanical beetle with antennae and six legs. The machine whirred for a few seconds and stopped short of the door.

'Can I have a go?' said Sean.

'Agent Lee, I have the results you were waiting for,' said Brown, speaking into his earpiece. 'And we have visitors. Hi, Major. And you must be Sean?'

Lee joined them, wearing a concerned look.

'Where's Mum?' said Sean.

'She's uh, resting. I'll wake her in a little while,' said Lee. 'She was…a little overexcited.'

Sean felt a hand on his shoulder. It was Clavity.

'I hope you have a good explanation?'

'She's a very determined lady,' said Lee. 'Anyway, we've made progress with our investigations.'

'Yes, we heard,' said Rusham.

Sean approached Lee and drew her gaze.

'So, why *did* Krankhausen steal my stuff?'

'We don't know,' said Lee. 'We're not even sure what he took.'

'A Dreampad, a pile of comics, and half my house,' said a voice behind them.

'Mum!' said Sean, rushing towards her.

Mrs Yeager was groggy and needed help to stand. To Sean's relief, she appeared calm.

'Where have you been, Sean? I've been worried sick.'

Sean was embarrassed but allowed himself to be hugged.

'We went after Krankhausen. He tried to blow us up, and

then we were attacked by a ferry and a shark. Eventually, a giant aircraft lifted us out of the sea. And I stayed at the Foundation's Headquarters last night.'

Mrs Yeager glared at Clavity.

'Our investigations will continue, Mrs Yeager,' said Clavity, still squelching in his shoes. 'Sean was quite safe. The recovery team arrived in next to no time.'

She gave Clavity a scowl that would wilt flowers at a hundred paces.

'Recovery team? Sharks?'

'Sorry,' said Clavity, squirming.

'Did you find your phone, Mum?' said Sean.

'No, but I remember answering it when I was tidying your room this morning. Or was it yesterday morning?'

'Perhaps you left it on my bed?' said Sean.

'It's possible, I suppose.'

Rusham stepped forwards.

'This could be important, Mrs Yeager. Can you please give me your phone number?'

Mrs Yeager dictated, and Rusham tapped the number into her mobile.

While Mrs Yeager caught up with Sean's news, Rusham took Clavity to one side.

'With any luck, Krankhausen stole the phone, and we can trace its signal.'

Clavity's eyes lit up. He tried to contact Cuthbertson, but his number was engaged.

'Confounded lock-down!'

****

Professor Quark knocked twice before bursting into Cuthbertson's private office. He closed the door behind him and surveyed the room as if expecting to find ninja warriors hiding in the corners. There were none.

'Professor, how can I help you?' said Cuthbertson, looking up from his paperwork.

Quark took a pen from Cuthbertson's desk and wrote a question on a notepad. It read: *Have you swept for bugs?*

Cuthbertson nodded.

'Good,' said Quark. 'I have a lot to tell you. We need to arrest Jenkins and put him in an isolation cell immediately.'

'But why? Jenkins has been working for the Foundation for as long as I can remember. He's our Head of Security!'

'He's also a mole,' said Quark. 'And I have the proof right here.'

Cuthbertson shook his head while Quark showed him a report of Jenkins' activities. It became clear that Jenkins had stolen a Matteract by forging three signatures, including those of Cuthbertson and Quark. Jenkins had accessed computer files he was not authorised to see and sent data outside of the Foundation. Quark played Cuthbertson a recording of a phone call he had intercepted.

'As I was saying, either you send me the passcodes I've requested, or you won't see your sister for a very long time. Do I make myself clear?' said a metallic voice.

'Yes, perfectly clear,' said Jenkins.

'Good,' said the caller.

Professor Quark stopped the recording and turned to Cuthbertson.

'According to our files, Jenkins has a sister who's been missing for several months. We believe she's being held for ransom by Krankhausen.'

Cuthbertson paused to consider this information.

'Jenkins? I can't believe it. Do we know where Krankhausen was calling from?'

'Alas no, he was careful to conceal his location as well as his voice,' said Quark. 'However, we did find a text message from Krankhausen on Jenkins' phone. We're working on a trace right now.'

Cuthbertson issued orders for Jenkins' arrest. Next, he asked Quark to prepare the mind-probe equipment. It would be hard on Jenkins, but what choice did they have? They needed information, and they needed it fast.

'What do we know about this Yeager boy?'

'Hardly anything,' said Quark. 'All Yeager's files are locked by the Founder himself.'

Cuthbertson tapped on his keyboard and searched for *Sean Yeager*. All he found was an address and a red label marked: *SP1*.

'I don't understand. Why would Krankhausen break into a boy's house?' said Cuthbertson. 'It makes no sense. And if *we* can't see his records, what has Jenkins discovered about Yeager?'

'I'll see what I can find out,' said Quark, rising to leave.

'Keep me informed, Professor.'

'Yes, of course.'

Cuthbertson checked his mobile phone. There were a few missed calls, including one from Clavity. However, he was in no hurry to speak to his field agents. After all, what had they achieved? They had damaged an expensive Foundation vehicle and lost all trace of Krankhausen. A pet dog would be more useful and cheaper to keep. However, Cuthbertson was worried. He remembered the St Jacobs incident, and there was no telling what Krankhausen might do next. The man was clearly deranged but also highly intelligent. Cuthbertson studied a map on his computer showing Krankhausen's most recent sightings.

'Where are you?'

He reached for his secure phone and speed dialled.

'Reynard? This is Cuthbertson.'

'Reynard here, sir.'

'Prepare Sigma Squad for a search mission.'

'Right away, sir. Where are we going?'

'Professor Quark will send you coordinates. We're on the hunt for Krankhausen.'

'And when we find him, sir?'

'Take him alive if you can, but I want his activities stopped.'

'Yes, sir. We'll do our best,' said Reynard.

'I'm sure you will. Good luck.'

****

'This lock-down is ridiculous!' said Rusham. 'Every phone I call is either engaged or switched off. Even Control!'

'I guess that's why they call it a *lock-down*,' said Clavity.

She had a point, though. How can you run an investigation if you can't call HQ for assistance? And if no one will lend you a vehicle? Agent Lee had also refused to help. She claimed her orders were to stay put and protect the Yeagers, which sounded strangely familiar.

'Have you tried calling your sweetheart?' said Clavity.

'Look, Major, he's *not* my sweetheart. I've told you a thousand times,' said Rusham, storming off.

'The lady doth protest too much, methinks,' whispered Clavity with a wry smile.

Rusham thumbed through her personal contacts and dialled.

'Captain Reynard? It's Elise, Elise Rusham.'

'Hello, Elise. I'm sorry, I'm busy right now.'

'Look, Captain, the thing is we've found a lead about you-know-who, and err…'

'Careful, this is an open line.'

'Yes, I know. I was wondering if you could arrange a lift for us?'

There was a long pause, and Rusham held her breath.

'I'm afraid that's impossible, Elise. I would risk being court-martialled.'

'Even if there was an agent in urgent need of medical attention?' said Rusham.

'Have you called Control?'

'I tried, but they're not answering.'

'And you're at the Yeager house?'

'Yes. We'll be waiting for you. Thank you, Captain.'

Reynard let out a sigh.

'I'll see what I can do, but I'm not making any promises.'

Rusham realised she had to work fast. She ran into the

house and found the medic. He was in the living room preparing to examine Mrs Yeager.

'Hi, I've heard you're a real hero,' said Rusham.

'Well, I err...do the best I can,' said the medic.

'I've been meaning to ask you, how do those knock-out devices work? They must be pretty dangerous in the wrong hands?'

'Not really,' said the medic.

He opened his case and produced a small, pen-like object. It was white with a button at one end and a round metallic bulb at the other.

'All you do is press the tip behind the subject's ear, and it sends them to sleep in an instant. It transmits a harmless, electrical pulse, which relaxes the patient's brain patterns.'

'Wow, that's amazing,' said Rusham. 'Can I have a look? I promise I'll be careful.'

The medic nodded and handed her the device.

'Where are you based?' said Rusham.

'HQ mostly. Although sometimes I'm posted to the Beach-hut or the Farmstead.'

'Must be interesting? Travelling all over the world?'

Rusham examined the device for a few seconds and pretended to drop it back into the case. If the medic had been watching more closely, he would have noticed Rusham distract his gaze at the critical time and drop a coin in its place.

'It has its moments,' said the medic.

'Oh, by the way, Mrs Yeager is still a bit wobbly. I think Agent Lee is worried about her.'

'Excuse me,' said the medic, picking up his case and hurrying to find them.

Rusham returned outside. She found Clavity examining a holographic reading of footprints.

'Major, have you seen Sean recently?'

'Yes, he's in the van. Why?'

'I think I've found us a lift.'

'With anyone I know?'

Rusham gave a faint smile.

'Sean's been looking pale since we brought him home, don't you think?'

'Has the medic checked him over?' said Clavity.

'I've asked him to, but he seems to have his hands full with Mrs Yeager. Besides, it could be something serious.'

Clavity grinned.

'Are you suggesting he needs to be airlifted to hospital by any chance, Agent Rusham?'

'It might be a good idea, sir. In the circumstances.'

'I like your thinking,' said Clavity, gesturing towards the driveway.

Inside the van, Sean was busy taking a spy-bot apart piece by piece. He followed instructions and removed a power cell from its casing.

'Well done, Sean. Good job,' said Brown.

Brown took the casing and held it up to a bench lamp. He tipped it back and forth to catch the light. As he did so, a layer of dark, metallic dust rolled around inside the plastic shell.

'Hi, Sean,' said Rusham. 'Have you figured it out yet?'

'Not quite.'

Brown looked up over his illuminated glasses.

'Their transformers were shorted out. It was probably caused by a power surge or an electromagnetic pulse.'

Clavity joined them and studied Sean's face.

'Hey, big guy, are you feeling okay? You're looking a bit pale.'

'You do seem a bit hot, Sean,' said Rusham, touching his brow. 'Major, what do you think?'

Clavity dabbed his hand on Sean's forehead. At the same time, Rusham reached behind Clavity's neck and tapped the sleep inducer under his ear. Clavity gave a brief murmur and slumped to one side.

'Major? Major!' said Rusham, hiding the device in her pocket.

'What's the matter?' said Brown.

'Major Clavity's collapsed!'

Brown helped to carry Clavity to the front of the van and laid him on a cushioned seat.

'Better fetch the medic,' said Brown. 'I'll see if I can reach Control. He might need an airlift.'

'Right away,' said Rusham, putting on her serious face.

A few minutes later, the medic appeared and examined Clavity. While he did so, Rusham edged closer and dropped the sleep inducer back into his case.

'He just fainted.'

The medic shook his head and took Clavity's pulse.

'I spoke to Captain Reynard,' said Rusham. 'He suggested we airlift Clavity to the Foundation Medical Centre.'

'That's probably a good idea,' said the medic. 'It could be a virus or a bug of some kind. Possibly even a heart attack. At his age, it's best not to take any chances.'

'Huh?' said Clavity, dribbling and half awake.

Several minutes later, a large shape covered the house in shadow. Shimmering, almost invisible against the sky, it hovered above the roof and made a loud whining sound. A door opened in mid-air, and two figures appeared wearing blue and grey camouflage.

Rusham's phone rang. It was Reynard.

'We need you to clear the front lawn.'

'Will do,' said Rusham, waving people towards the house. A bright-orange stretcher fell from the sky. It bounced on a pair of cables and came to rest on the grass. The medic stepped forwards and set to work undoing its harnesses while Brown helped Clavity from the van.

'There's no way I'm going anywhere in that!' cried Mrs Yeager from the doorway.

'It's not for you. It's for Major Clavity,' said Lee.

Meanwhile, Clavity staggered across the lawn.

'I am not an invalid,' he said, almost collapsing on the grass. 'I *can* walk, you know?'

Rusham called Reynard.

'Do you have any harnesses?'

A figure high above gave a thumbs-up, and two bright orange, padded harnesses fell to the ground bringing lines with them. Brown and the medic helped Clavity secure one of them around his body and signalled to the waiting crew.

While Clavity was being winched skywards, Sean hurried to the van. He picked up a repaired spy-bot and taped two aerosol cans to its shell so that they dangled behind its legs. He carried the spy-bot to the far side of the plastic tunnel and activated it by following Brown's instructions. At once, the mechanical insect whirred and clattered its way across the driveway, dragging the cans and making an almighty din.

Sean heard startled voices and sprinted back to the van. Agent Rusham was already in mid-air, and the lawn was deserted. He crept to the discarded stretcher, strapped himself in, and pulled an orange blanket over his body.

'Don't leave without me,' he whispered and crossed his fingers for luck.

Sure enough, after a few seconds, the stretcher became airborne. From under the blanket, Sean watched inquisitive faces appear at a neighbours' window and was tempted to wave. The stretcher swayed above the rooftops, and Sean laughed at a pair of startled birds as they flew by. Eventually, he reached an opening in the sky, and the stretcher was hauled inside a cargo bay. Sean lay concealed under the blanket and waited. Before long, a hatch slammed shut, and with a thunderous roar, the Skyraptor powered away across the sky.

CHAPTER 8: HUNTING NEEDLES

Sean peeked out from under his blanket. A solitary bulb bathed the cargo bay in pale, yellow light, and there was an acrid smell of metal and oil. Once Sean's eyes had adjusted, he noticed the fuselage was constructed of metal ribs covered in grey padding, pipes, and wires. Everything around him rattled and shook like a tumble dryer. He rose from the stretcher and hid behind some cargo boxes lashed to the floor.

'How's our patient?' said a uniformed figure in a raised voice.

'Major Clavity seems fine to me,' said another, wearing a serpent and stick badge on his sleeve. 'I don't know why we're taking him to HQ.'

'I guess it's a precaution.'

'The Brigadier's not going to be happy.'

'Tell me about it.'

Rusham helped Clavity up a metal staircase to the flight deck. Reynard waved them into a cabin and slid a door behind them, blocking out most of the noise. Inside the cabin, a uniformed navigator studied a large holographic map.

'What is it you have to tell me?' said Reynard.

Rusham helped Clavity to a seat before answering.

'We have the number of a mobile phone we believe Krankhausen may have stolen.'

Reynard stared at Rusham for a moment as if waiting for more information. When none was offered, he burst into laughter.

'A phone number? Is that all? Here, let me show you something.'

He led them to the holographic map and pointed at a vast area of pale blue. A wide scattering of dots stretched around a label that read: *Hermes*.

'You see this? We have thousands of square miles of ocean to search and only six aircraft,' said Reynard.

Rusham nodded.

'We have hundreds of targets to investigate, and every one of them is moving. Now, do you see a single phone mast on this map?'

'What about satellites?' said Rusham. 'I thought you could phone anywhere these days?'

'Sure, if Krankhausen has a satellite uplink *just* to answer this phone of yours,' said Reynard.

Rusham sighed and looked up at the ceiling. She felt frustrated and humiliated. But there was still a nagging question eating away inside her.

'We'll take Major Clavity to HQ and continue our search,' said Reynard.

'You see, the thing is...' said Rusham, pausing to choose her words.

Reynard waited as if daring Rusham to finish her sentence. During the stand-off, the navigator approached.

'Yes, Sebastian?' said Reynard.

'If the phone is *on*, we can locate its signal using two of our transmitters, sir.'

'Do we have suitable transmitters?'

'Yes, sir. All Skyraptors can send and receive mobile phone signals, but we'll need the right software to mimic the phone's network.'

Reynard paced the room for a few moments, deep in thought. He surveyed the maps and eyed Rusham with a look of amused respect.

'Sebastian, call Control and ask for their help.'

'You'll need this,' said Rusham, proudly displaying a phone number on her smartphone.

Reynard's earpiece beeped. He answered it and grinned at Clavity.

'It seems, Major, that you have made a miraculous recovery.'

'We were just being cautious,' said Rusham.

'Tell me more, Agent Rusham.'

Before she could reply, a voice crackled on a nearby speaker.

'It's Recon-one, sir,' said Sebastian.

'Patch them through,' said Reynard.

'Go ahead, Recon-one.'

'We have visual contact with Tango-one-niner. It's a cargo ship, over.'

'Roger that, Recon-one. Proceed to Tango-two-zero,' said Sebastian.

The navigator tapped the report into a keyboard, and one of the hundreds of shapes on the map changed from blue to green. He waited for a response, but there was only static.

'Recon-one, this is Sunbeam, do you copy?'

Again there was no reply. Seconds later, the speaker burst into life.

'Mayday! Mayday! This is Recon-one. We are under attack! Repeat, we are under attack!'

There was shocked silence in the room.

'Recon-one, who is attacking you?' said Reynard.

But there was no reply.

'Where are they?' said Reynard.

'About here, sir,' said Sebastian, indicating a flashing red shape on one of the maps.

The symbol hovered over deep water, miles from shore.

'Change our heading. We're going to assist,' said Reynard. 'I'm going back to the flight deck. Strap in, everyone. This could be a bumpy ride.'

On the flight deck, the crew was tense. No one could understand how it was possible to detect a Foundation Raptor, let alone shoot one down. Reynard ordered Skyraptor-one's stealth device to be activated as a precaution. In theory, they should be invisible to enemy radar, but then so should every other Foundation aircraft.

Clavity felt better and went in search of a restroom. He found one on the cargo deck and reached for a door handle.

As he did so, the door slid open to reveal Sean with a look of horror on his face.

'What are *you* doing here?' said Clavity.

Sean blushed.

'Going after Krankhausen. Isn't that the plan?'

Clavity shook his head.

'You're incorrigible, Master Yeager. May I?'

Reynard gazed out at the ocean. He sat behind the pilot and co-pilot and next to the radar operator. In front of him, a screen showed possible targets on a circular grid. It displayed a red blip where Recon-one had been.

'Sunbeam, this is Control. Recon-one is heading back to base. We believe their transmitter malfunctioned, over.'

'Roger that, Control. Request permission to engage Tango-one-niner, over.'

'This is Brigadier Cuthbertson. You have permission to disable Tango One Nine, but only if fired upon, over.'

'Understood, Brigadier,' said Reynard, rubbing his hands together.

Clavity led Sean to the navigation room.

'Look who I've found.'

'Sean? What are you doing here?' said Rusham.

The room was filled with radio noise, and the navigator clenched his fist.

'What's going on?' said Sean.

'We're going after a hostile ship,' said Rusham.

'With Sean on board?' said Clavity.

Rusham and Clavity exchanged bemused looks.

'Reynard's in charge now,' said Rusham, in a carefree tone.

'And I'm sure you'll both be very happy,' said Clavity, winking.

Rusham scowled.

'I got us a lift, didn't I?'

The map table flashed a rectangular symbol enclosed by a shape resembling a red cross-hair.

'Time to strap in, Sean,' said Clavity, indicating a spare seat. 'We're going fishing again.'

'I hope you know what you're doing this time?'

Rusham grinned.

'Care to comment, Major?'

'Don't bring me into this,' said Clavity, 'I'm only a passenger.'

Sean laughed.

Moments later, alarms rang out across the flight deck, and a grey and white ship appeared on the horizon.

'Captain, we have missiles locked onto us and in-flight,' said Radar.

'Impossible!' said Reynard. 'We're in stealth mode.'

'Tracking two missiles. Estimated impact in thirty seconds, Captain, stealth mode or otherwise.'

'Weapons, activate lasers and counter-measures,' said Reynard. 'Comms, jam their signals. Flight, take evasive action!'

Skyraptor-one climbed and turned sharply left. Its engines flared with afterburners. As it accelerated, its wings swept back and carved vapour trails through the air.

'Impact in twenty seconds,' said Radar, straining against the g-force.

'Lasers are locked on and firing,' said Weapons.

The missiles changed direction and raced after them. Skyraptor-one fled vertically, its laser turrets flashing beams of red in its wake. The first laser struck the nose cone of a missile which promptly exploded; while the second missed its target altogether and boiled a patch of seawater far below.

'There's a missile on our tail!' said Radar.

'Counter-measures away,' said Flight.

Skyraptor-one shed a cloud of tiny metal pieces on silver parachutes. As they fell, they spread out and exploded like fireworks as the Raptor soared ever higher. The second missile sped into the debris.

'Boom!'

'The second missile has detonated,' said Radar.

'Right, let's find the hostile ship,' said Reynard.

'Levelling out, sir,' said Flight.

Two miles above the sea, Skyraptor-one slowed and adjusted its wings. It cruised above the clouds and scanned the ocean.

'We have contact with Tango-one-niner,' said Radar.

Reynard considered his options. He knew it would be easy to destroy a cargo ship, but how could they disable one? A missile or laser strike could make the whole vessel explode, particularly if it was carrying missiles. Reynard ruled out a direct attack.

'Prepare two EMP mines for a medium-distance ignition.'

'Yes, sir,' said Weapons.

'Flight, plot a course for a high-speed bombing approach.'

'Yes, sir.'

Skyraptor-one descended and approached its target in a wide circle. Ten nautical miles from the cargo ship, it dipped below the clouds and accelerated to supersonic speed.

'We've identified the contact,' said Radar. 'The target is confirmed as Tango-one-niner.'

'Systems are locked-on, sir,' said Weapons.

'Launch EMP mines when ready,' said Reynard.

'Automated launch is ready, sir.'

'Carry on, Weapons,' said Reynard.

Before the cargo ship could sound an alarm, Skyraptor-one had raced overhead. Two guided bombs landing in the ocean on either side of the vessel. They exploded in small mushroom clouds and sent shock waves in every direction. Electromagnetic radiation swept through the cargo ship, and electricity sparked in every piece of metal it contained. Radars, missiles, and transmitters blew their circuits. Computers overloaded and all their lights went out. The ship slowed and began to drift on the waves, miles from anywhere.

'Tango-one-niner is damaged, sir. It's lost power,' said Radar.

'Good work, team,' said Reynard. 'Comms, report the target's location and status to HQ.'

'Will do, sir.'

'Perhaps the Brigadier himself will pay them a visit?' said Reynard, barely disguising a grin.

CHAPTER 9: DAMAGE

The Foundation's Control Centre buzzed with activity. Screens flashed and keyboards were pounded as Foundation agents did their best to locate Krankhausen. Reports flooded in from aircraft of all shapes and sizes and filled the room with radio chatter. Professor Quark climbed a short flight of steps to the inner sanctum.

'Brigadier, I have grave news.'

'What is it, Professor?'

'I've been reviewing the findings from Jenkins' mind probe. We've found evidence he's been leaking secrets to Krankhausen for months. There were also strange puncture marks on the back of his neck.'

Cuthbertson groaned. The situation was worse than he feared. He had never really liked Jenkins, but he had a begrudging respect for the man and his in-depth knowledge of security matters.

'Jenkins also managed to ship several Foundation weapons abroad disguised as machine parts.'

'Do we know what they were?' said Cuthbertson.

Quark puffed out his cheeks.

'They could have been almost anything. Jenkins even gained access to some of our secret research projects.'

Cuthbertson stared at the ceiling. A minor burglary had turned into a crisis. Recon-one was limping back to base, and the enemy missile ship had somehow vanished. Reynard was hunting an invisible madman. To make matters worse, it now appeared that Krankhausen was armed to the teeth with the Foundation's own weapons.

'What about this Sean Yeager? Have you managed to find out why he's a priority-one subject?'

Quark wiped his glasses before answering.

'All his files are locked and encrypted. However, the Founder books him a medical every year.'

'We all have medicals,' said Cuthbertson.

'Of course, but you should see the list of procedures. Sean has every scan, measurement, and test you can imagine. And a lot more besides.'

'I don't understand,' said Cuthbertson. 'Why would the Founder be so interested in Yeager's health?'

'I wonder,' said Quark. 'Perhaps he's Sean's guardian?'

Cuthbertson paled. It was beginning to come back to him now. Mrs Yeager had lost her partner during a Foundation mission, and the Founder had promised to protect her for life. In effect, the Founder *was* looking after the boy. Cuthbertson rose and addressed everyone in the Control Centre.

'Can anyone tell me where Sean Yeager is right now?'

Every agent in the room studied their screens and pretended to be busy. Cuthbertson glanced at Quark, who gave a pained expression.

'No! Don't tell me he's with…'

Quark gave a pained look.

'Get me Reynard this instant!'

****

Egbert Von Krankhausen prowled the main deck of his new premises like a predator spoiling for a fight. It was an impressive structure anchored in the middle of the ocean. He gazed out at the horizon through an expanse of tinted glass and rubbed his nose thoughtfully.

The main deck was a large and comfortable space containing plants, sofas, and an impressive array of hi-tech equipment. On one side of the room, a row of technicians worked at a bank of screens. Greerbo stood behind them, offering snarls of encouragement. His style of leadership was unpopular, to say the least.

'Where are they, Greerbo?' said Krankhausen. 'I want to see them explode in front of me.'

'They've evaded our missile ships, boss.'

'Pah! Enough of these games! Launch the Paladins.'

'You heard the man!'

The white coats scurried into action and lit up another row of consoles.

'Boss, what shall I do about Jenkins?'

Krankhausen's lips stretched into a thin smile.

'Trigger his implants. Jenkins could become a most valuable asset.'

****

Sean was bored and tapped his feet against the metal floor. Skyraptor-one had been circling for ages, and there was still no sign of Krankhausen. He listened to reports as they came in. Foundation patrols had identified cruise liners, ferries, cargo ships, and pleasure boats, but nothing suspicious. If Krankhausen was out there, he was well hidden.

'Shall we take a look at the flight deck?' said Clavity.

'Can we?' said Sean excitedly.

'I'm coming with you,' said Rusham.

The three passengers filed along a narrow corridor. Clavity reached a bulkhead door and heaved it open. They entered a hive of activity bathed in bright sunlight. An expanse of switches and lights stretched out before them, and dozens of screens flickered with information. Through the cockpit windows, Sean noticed a perfect blue sky resting on a carpet of fluffy, white clouds.

'I'd forgotten you were on board,' said Reynard, spinning around in his chair. 'And what is this young man doing on *my* Raptor?'

Sean stepped forwards and offered his hand.

'Sean Yeager, pleased to meet you.'

'Pleased to meet you, young man,' said Reynard, returning the gesture. 'And what do you think of our flight deck?'

'It's amazing!' said Sean, his eyes wide.

Reynard studied him with a look of suspicion.

'And how exactly did you manage to board this Raptor?'

Clavity intervened to deflect the question.

'Any sign of Krankhausen? We must be running low on fuel by now?'

Reynard glanced at a nearby screen and smiled.

'Major, we have enough fuel to run our micro-fusion engines for days. However, Krankhausen still eludes us. But you didn't answer my question. Sean…'

Sean closed his eyes and began to shake.

'Are you okay?' said Rusham

'We need to get anyway from here.'

'Why? There's nothing up here but clouds and sky.'

Sean's face drained of colour.

'Something terrible is coming.'

'What do you mean?'

'They're angry. Really angry.'

A nearby member of crew flicked a switch and answered a call.

'Captain, it's HQ. Brigadier Cuthbertson wants to speak to you urgently.'

'Go ahead, Control,' said Reynard, rotating his chair. He took the call and span around with a grave expression.

'Major, we are to return Sean Yeager to HQ at once. The Brigadier is very upset.'

Clavity frowned.

'But surely he's in safe hands?'

'And what about the phone?' said Rusham.

An orange light flashed, and two blips appeared on a tracking screen.

'Captain, we have two incoming contacts.'

'What's their heading?' said Reynard.

'They're coming straight at us,' said Radar. 'No, they can't be!'

'Can't be what?' said Reynard.

'The contacts are travelling at Mach 5, sir.'

The tracking screen went blank. Radar tapped some controls and shook her head.

'Control, this is Sunbeam; please confirm our satellite link

70

is working?'

'Sunbeam, this is Control. We've lost you on our tracking system. Take extreme caution, over.'

'Is there a problem?' said Reynard.

Before Radar could reply, a booming voice rattled the speakers.

'This is Cuthbertson. Leave the area immediately. Repeat, leave the...'

Cuthbertson's voice trailed off in a wail of static.

'What's happening, Comms?' said Reynard.

'We've lost contact with Control, sir.'

Reynard pulled a face and tapped commands into his own screen.

There was a huge roar outside, and two small aircraft raced past. They sped into the distance and became tiny dots in seconds. Just as quickly, the aircraft returned, and there was a brilliant flash of light as they roared overhead.

'What are those things?' said Reynard.

'We've been hit, sir!' said Flight. 'On our starboard wing.'

'I can't see anything on radar, sir.'

'Our defences are active,' said Weapons. 'But we can't seem to lock onto them.'

'Flight, get us into the clouds!' said Reynard. 'We're a sitting duck up here.'

At once, the deck sloped sharply forwards.

'Grab hold of something!' cried Rusham

Sean scrambled to an empty seat and groaned as his hip struck a metal edge. The Skyraptor continued to dive, and Sean became pinned against a map table. Rusham dragged him across the deck, and they leaned on a metal panel, straining against gravity. Meanwhile, Clavity flew headlong into the rear of Reynard's seat and struck his head. Sean glanced at his slumped body and noticed blood trickling from Clavity's motionless forehead.

Skyraptor-one levelled out inside a bank of dense clouds and slowed down. There were further roars outside as the enemy aircraft buzzed them, but this time there were no flashes.

'Damage report?' said Reynard.

'All systems are operational, sir. Micro-bots are repairing the damage to our wing,' said Flight.

'I've never seen anything fly so fast. Any ideas?' said Reynard.

Sean picked himself up and joined Rusham, who was kneeling beside Clavity.

'There's no one on those planes,' said Sean, within earshot of Reynard.

'Impossible!' said Reynard. 'They *must* have pilots.'

'I'm not picking up any life signs,' said Radar.

'He could be right, sir,' said Flight. 'We were testing a high-speed stealth drone at the Farmstead only last spring.'

'What?' said Reynard. 'Why wasn't I informed?'

'It was a classified project, sir.'

Reynard let out a snort of disdain.

'And if they *are* drones, how do we stop them? Or is that classified too?'

'We need to jam their control signals,' said Radar. 'They're like remote control toys, only bigger and faster.'

'Were you at the Farmstead as well?' said Reynard.

'Not as such,' said Radar, blushing.

'Right, let's do it. Weapons, can you shoot them down?'

'Not in this fog, sir. It's blocking our targeting systems. We need a clear line of sight.'

'Ready to scan for the targets' control signal, sir,' said Radar.

'Meaning?'

'We need them to buzz us again so we can detect the frequency they're operating on.'

'Mer…credi!' said Reynard. 'We have to offer ourselves to these wolves like a helpless lamb?'

'It's the only way, sir,' said Radar.

While Reynard made his decision, Rusham tended to Clavity's wound with the help of a first aid pack. He was awake but shaken, and his forehead needed stitches. Rusham put a field dressing over his eye and did her best to clean his face. Sean helped by passing sterile wipes and cotton wool swabs.

'Right,' said Reynard, 'let's take out these drones.'

Sean trembled at the thought of confronting the enemy aircraft, and his stomach churned.

'Weapons, prepare heat-seeking missiles. Flight, I want to be skimming the clouds, no higher.'

Skyraptor-one rose out of the fog and waited. Another loud roar announced the return of the drones. They streaked overhead from tail to nose, firing as they went. Once they had passed, there were bursts of flames from underneath the Skyraptor, and missiles raced after them.

'I have their frequencies,' said Radar. 'Jamming the drone's control signals now.'

The drones turned and sped back towards them. The first flew straight into the path of a pursuing missile and exploded. However, the second continued on a collision course.

'It's coming straight at us!' said Flight, dipping Skyraptor-one's nose at the last second.

The drone thundered past, missing them by the smallest of margins, and flew on in a straight line. A third missile followed in its wake.

'Missile in-flight and locked-on,' said Weapons. 'Contact in…a few minutes.'

'Minutes?' said Reynard.

'We've lost it. The target is out of range, sir,' said Radar.

'Our missile is self-destructing,' said Weapons.

'Daileeshphi!' said Reynard, slamming his fist against his chair.

Rusham gave a surprised look.

'Temper, temper,' she whispered.

****

Jenkins woke in a cell at Foundation HQ. He wore a one-piece overall and discovered his glasses and personal effects were missing. Jenkins remembered feeling uneasy and being wheeled into a room that resembled an operating theatre. Afterwards, he had no idea what happened. Perhaps he had dreamt the whole thing? But that would not explain his predicament.

Jenkins paced the cell and began to feel anxious. His head span with strange images, and his heart beat wildly. In his mind's eye, he saw pictures of a house in flames. It was his sister's house. Weapons were fired outside, and the building erupted into an inferno. It was Cuthbertson's fault, he reasoned. Who else could have ordered these things? Jenkins began to shake with anger. He felt a surge of hatred build inside him and staggered to his meagre bed. His body throbbed, and his vision turned red.

'You'll pay for what you've done!' he cried and keeled over on the mattress, shaking.

Greaves was passing in the corridor outside and heard Jenkins moaning. He squinted through an eyeglass in the cell door and was alarmed by what he saw. The prisoner was curled up on a bed, shaking from head to toe. His face was flushed, and his mouth was wide open. Jenkins clawed at the air above him as if trying to fight off an unseen attacker. Greaves pressed a panic button on the wall and spoke into his earpiece.

'Pearson! Craddock! Call the medics. Jenkins is having a fit! And suit up, you're coming in with me.'

He set his baton to stun and went in search of a helmet and protective collar. He'd seen it all before. These crazies were capable of anything. His colleagues arrived in full riot gear, eager for a scrap.

'Pearson, fetch the cradle. We're going to strap him in and wheel him down to the sickbay, understood?'

'Yes, sir.'

Greaves opened the cell door and edged towards the prisoner. Jenkins seemed unaware of his presence and continued to battle his invisible demons. In the meantime,

Pearson wheeled in the restraining cradle. Greaves pointed at Jenkins' legs, following a drill they had practiced a hundred times before. Pearson and Craddock gave a thumbs-up. They inched forwards and pounced, each grabbing an ankle. Greaves stood over Jenkins, ready to zap him unconscious at the first sign of trouble.

However, Jenkins had other ideas. He kicked both legs upwards and knocked Pearson and Craddock flying into the wall. In one movement, he arched his back like a gymnast and rose into a handstand. Greaves caught him with a glancing bolt of electricity, but it had little effect. Jenkins tumbled head over heels and twisted in the air. In a panic, Greaves aimed for his neck but missed. Now Jenkins was upon him. He struck Greaves firmly in the stomach and made him double up on the floor before wrenching the baton from his grasp.

Pearson and Craddock recovered and blocked Jenkins' path to the door. They drew batons and stood shoulder to shoulder, ready for a scrap. Jenkins let out a snarl and charged at them. He hurled his weapon. It sparked and struck Craddock squarely in the chest a fraction of a second before his Jenkins arrived. He bowled Craddock over like an electrocuted skittle and landed on top of him. Meantime, Pearson grabbed hold of Jenkins' arm and tried to wrestle him to the ground. However, the prisoner twisted under his grasp and swept Pearson's legs out from underneath him. He rolled and fired at Jenkins' head but only succeeded in melting a ceiling light and plunging the cell into darkness.

Greaves struggled to his feet in time to see Jenkins sprint away into the corridor, cackling at his regained freedom. Greaves activated his earpiece.

'Control? We have a prisoner on the loose. Lock down the cell block, and seal the guardroom.'

There was a muffled sound of laughter.

'Have you been jumped again, Greaves?' said Control.

'Knock it off, will you? The prisoner is armed and dangerous. Approach him with extreme caution.'

'Do you need some help down there?'

Greaves watched Pearson and Craddock clamber gingerly to their feet. He was sorely tempted to agree.

'No, it's nothing we can't handle,' he said and switched off his earpiece.

'I bet he's heading to the armoury,' said Pearson.

'Yes, and next time we'll be ready for him,' said Greaves.

CHAPTER 10: GAMBLE

Greerbo was in a foul mood and stabbed the controls of his drone in frustration. An enemy aircraft was at his mercy, and all he had to do was aim and fire. Greerbo moved in for the kill and squeezed the trigger. He expected the Paladin's laser cannons to flash in front of him, but nothing happened.

'Who's been meddling with my controls?' They should be in pieces by now!'

A frightened technician beside him studied a screen and shook her head in disbelief.

'There's nothing wrong. Your Paladin's in perfect condition.'

'Then why won't it fire?' said Greerbo, letting out a snarl.

He wrestled the controls, but the Paladin refused to respond.

'Someone's jamming our signals,' said the technician.

'Then do something! Boost them!'

Greerbo's video feed went blank, and the technician's shoulders slumped. The drone, or what was left of it, had fallen into the ocean.

'Try Paladin Two. I think it's still responding,' said the technician, backing away.

Greerbo grunted and approached the pilot of the second drone. He pushed his chair so hard, it span away across the room and struck the edge of a table. The chair deposited the startled pilot on the floor. He was about to complain when he saw the look of thunder on Greerbo's face. Instead, the pilot crept away to a safe distance.

'Useless!' said Greerbo. 'This one's broken as well.'

'What is it, Greerbo?' said an insistent voice.

Krankhausen approached flanked on either side by an armed guard.

'The Paladins are failing us, boss.'

'The Paladins or our *pilots*?' said Krankhausen. 'I've given you the best equipment the world has to offer, and you haven't managed to shoot down *one* Foundation aircraft!'

'Guards! Take him away!' said Krankhausen, pointing at the startled ex-pilot of Paladin Two.

The pilot considered running, but the guards closed in and drew their weapons.

'And Greerbo, I expect better from you. You must redouble your efforts. Order our missile ships to shoot down those Foundation idiots.'

'Right away, boss.'

'And I want Jenkins activated at once. His mission is to destroy the Foundation's Headquarters. He'll enjoy that. If he survives.'

'And then what?' said Greerbo.

'And then nothing. Jenkins will be of no further use to us,' said Krankhausen, with a cruel smile.

'Yes, boss,' said Greerbo. 'I won't fail you.'

'True,' said Krankhausen. 'Nobody fails me for long. Guards, show this gentleman the way out.'

The pilot struggled free of his captors and ran for an exit.

'Don't just stand there!' said Krankhausen, gesturing to the guards. 'He has an appointment with the bottom of the ocean!'

****

Skyraptor-one had been circling in cloud cover for some time. Its wings were spread wide, and it scanned the sea and sky for threats. Beneath its outer skin, micro-bots repaired a damaged wing strut. It was a slow job.

'Any sign of the second drone?' said Reynard.

'Nothing, sir,' said Radar.

'Have you managed to locate the source of its control signal?'

'I've tried, sir, but the signals are coming from hundreds of locations. Their echoing across a hundred-mile radius.'

'He's down there somewhere. I can feel it in my bones.'

Reynard considered his options. They could return to HQ or continue their search for Krankhausen. He dearly wanted to teach Krankhausen a lesson, and it would not be in diplomacy.

'Sir, we have incoming messages from our recon flights. They're requesting permission to return to base for re-fuelling,' said Comms.

'Permission granted,' said Reynard. 'Tell them to stay alert in case any more drones turn up.'

'Yes, sir,' said Comms, typing the message.

Sean rose from his chair and approached Reynard.

'I know where Krankhausen is.'

'You do?' said Reynard, raising his eyebrows.

'He's waiting for us down there,' said Sean, pointing to a stretch of sea on their left.

'But how can you know this, Sean?' said Reynard. 'Krankhausen is probably thousands of miles away by now.'

'I get these feelings,' said Sean hesitantly.

'Feelings?' said Reynard. 'But do you have any evidence?'

Rusham left her nursing duties and joined them.

'We could always try the phone?'

Reynard screwed up his face as if he had bitten a slice of lemon.

'Alright, Agent Rusham, I give in. We will test this theory of yours.'

'Comms, contact Skyraptor-two and prepare to call this mobile phone,' said Reynard, smirking.

'Will do, sir. It will take about five minutes to set up the transmission.'

Reynard turned to Sean with a twinkle in his eye.

'So, Master Sean, what do your feelings tell you about this plan of ours?'

Sean stared into the distance.

'It depends.'

'On what?'

'On when *they* arrive.'

Reynard gave a quizzical expression.

79

'Our transmitters are ready, sir,' said Comms.

'Okay, call the number,' said Reynard.

'The phone is ringing now, sir.'

Reynard sighed to himself. He suspected the phone had been left on a shop counter somewhere by a distracted mother. It would either ring unanswered or divert to voicemail. No matter, at least it would keep Rusham quiet for a while. However, Sean's answer concerned him.

****

In an empty laboratory, Willard inspected a row of cloudy test tubes.

'What's the matter with you? Separate, damn you!'

He watched a batch of hair samples cook in a chemical soup. Meanwhile, the rest of the hair had been cleaned and stored as instructed by Krankhausen. In normal circumstances, he would have several thousand copies of DNA by now. However, this DNA refused to be copied, and he had no choice but to start again.

Willard was worried. Not about the DNA, so what if it was abnormal? His biggest and ugliest concern was Greerbo. That animal needed to be kept in a cage, preferably underwater. Which reminded him—he needed to feed Krankhausen's latest experiment, and he would have to endure that awful stench.

Willard went through a mental checklist. His equipment was all in order, but he realised he had forgotten to chill any alcohol. Willard clapped his hands together in frustration. How many times had he performed this procedure? Willard opened a cupboard and hauled out a Winchester full of ethanol. As ever, its weight caught him by surprise. He set it on a workbench and went in search of a measuring tube. As Willard began to pour the liquid, a buzzing sound and music echoed across the lab. He spilled ethanol on his fingers and cursed. It started to evaporate, and the technician hurried to wash his hands under a tap. He hated the way alcohol dried and cracked his skin.

The noise stopped, and Willard relaxed. He had just covered his hands in soap when music rang out again from a bench on the far side of the laboratory.

'How am I expected to work in these conditions?'

Willard stomped over to the bench. He rummaged through a collection of children's belongings and discovered a silver mobile phone. It continued to buzz and play music in his wet, soapy hand.

'Can't you see I'm busy?' he cried and threw it across the laboratory.

The phone flashed and buzzed on its short journey across a workbench. It struck the back of a metal chair and bounced. Turning end over end, it clattered on the rim of a centrifuge and came to rest upside down against a gas tap. However, the phone continued to ring.

'How dare you?' cried Willard.

He stormed across the room and pounded the phone with his fist. Its screen shattered, and his second blow silenced it. Willard picked the phone up between two fingers and dropped it into a yellow bin labelled *Hazardous Waste*.

'Ha! You disgusting machine. Try disturbing me from the incinerator!' he said and stomped away to finish his work.

And then the phone clicked and disconnected.

****

On the flight deck of Skyraptor-one, Sean listened to a dialling tone. It rang and rang, unanswered.

'No response, sir,' said Comms.

'Try it again,' said Reynard, glancing at Rusham.

Comms tapped instructions into a computer, and the dialling tones returned.

'Ringing now, sir.'

'Beep, beep! Beep, beep! Beep, beep!'

'As I thought,' said Reynard. 'It's not even going to voicemail.'

Sean watched Rusham and Clavity strain to hear the dialling tones. They reminded him of anxious parents at a school play. All of a sudden, there was a sharp click on the monitor.

'Hello? Who is this? Sean, is that you?'

It was a female voice. Agent Rusham turned to Sean.

'Is that your mother?' she whispered.

He gave a grave nod.

'Sorry, wrong number,' said Reynard and hung up.

He turned in triumph to Rusham and grinned. Just then, a message flashed up in red on Reynard's screen.

'Incoming encrypted message for you, sir,' said Comms.

Reynard tapped his screen and shook his head.

'Agent Rusham, are you in league with Professor Quark?'

'Err, no. What makes you think that?'

Reynard typed some numbers into his personal console.

'Comms, we have a new number to call. Apparently, everyone has the same idea today.'

'Dialling now, sir.'

Again there were sounds of a ring tone. This time, a muffled click was followed by static and a distant voice.

'What was that?' said Rusham.

'It sounded like: *you disgusting machine*,' said Sean.

'It sounded like gold dust to me!' said Clavity.

'Do we have a fix on the phone's signal?' said Reynard.

'Yes, sir!' said two voices together.

'On display now,' said Radar.

The main screen showed an area of the Atlantic covered by hundreds of orange dots. In the lower quarter, a solitary dot flashed green. Reynard rubbed his hands together.

'Comms, patch me through to Skyraptor-two. We have a criminal to catch.'

Clavity gave Rusham a thumbs-up, and she put on her *I told you so* look.

'This is Reynard, all crew to attack stations!' He turned to Clavity. 'And that includes our stowaways. Jump to it!'

Rusham approached Reynard's chair.

'What did you say about phone masts?'

Reynard gave a sheepish grin.

'We can celebrate your hunch when our mission is complete. But remember, it was not your number.'

'Promises, promises,' said Clavity.

Sean felt a dread deep inside. He knew something evil lay in the ocean and sensed three soulless eyes watching their every move.

'They're waiting for us,' he whispered.

****

Jenkins reached a storage cupboard and slipped inside. It was packed with cleaning equipment. He flicked on a light switch and discovered a cart laden with bottles, an array of mops, and cloths. Jenkins jammed the door shut using a mop handle and glanced up. In the ceiling was an air vent fronted by a metal grille. Visions again filled his head. He saw bonfires, gas stoves, and flames. In his twisted mind, everything in the cupboard became fuel.

'You had this coming, Brigadier!'

Jenkins piled rags and cloths on the floor and soaked them in cleaning fluid. The smell almost made him choke. He moved the cart under the air vent and climbed up to reach the grill. It cut into his fingers, and specks of blood splattered on the floor. However, Jenkins felt nothing but an unstoppable rage. Rooting around in the back of the cupboard, he found a tray of rusty tools. He selected a screwdriver and returned to unfasten the grill. After some frantic unscrewing, it crashed to the floor. Jenkins rose and gazed inside. It was a route he knew well from studying plans of the building, but would the air duct hold his weight? There was only one way to find out.

Voices and footsteps sounded in the corridor. The door handle rattled. Orders were barked, and someone started pounding on the cupboard door. Jenkins wrapped his hand in a cloth and tugged at the light fitting. The ceiling cracked, and the glass bulb smashed on the floor. The light went out, but the lightbulb's glowing filament landed in a puddle of cleaning fluid.

'Woof!'

In an instant, fire streaked across the liquid and reached the rags. They smouldered before catching fire and filling the cupboard with smoke.

Several guards gathered in the corridor. They took turns hitting the cupboard door with anything they could find. They discovered that fire extinguishers were more effective than shoulders and feet, but the door remained intact.

'Stand aside!' said a figure, dressed in grey and blue body armour.

A commando drew a blaster from his holster, selected a heat setting, and fired. The door handle glowed orange, and the surrounding wood charred. The commando picked up a discarded fire extinguisher and smashed it against the handle. Its lock snapped, and the door swung open. An instant later, the commando was blown off his feet by a blast of flames from inside the cupboard. He landed on his back with his boots in the air.

'Shall we use it properly this time?' said Greaves, picking up the dented fire extinguisher and pointing it at the flames.

A series of piercing fire alarms rang out across the building, and water sprinklers doused the corridor in a dense mist. While Greaves put out the blaze, Jenkins crawled away through the air vent. One step closer to his target.

CHAPTER 11: ASSAULT

The Control Centre at Foundation HQ was in disarray. Its satellite links were broken, and Cuthbertson had no way of contacting Reynard. There were puddles in the cellblock corridor, and acrid smoke had spread throughout the East Wing. The fire was out, but Jenkins was proving difficult to track down. Even with video cameras, spy-bots, and guards in pursuit. However, the fire alarms were at last silent.

Brigadier Cuthbertson accepted a phone call from Greaves.

'Let me get this straight,' said Cuthbertson. 'Jenkins has gone crazy. He's escaped into an air vent, and he's trying to burn down the building?'

'Yes, sir. We think he's heading to the armoury.'

Cuthbertson turned to Professor Quark for reassurance.

'Is there any way Jenkins can get into the armoury?'

'He would need to reach the main lift shaft,' said Quark, frowning.

The consequences of a maniac letting off weapons inside the Foundation's armoury did not bear thinking about. It held missiles and grenades amongst other things. An explosion could cause a chain reaction that would wipe the whole building off the face of the planet.

'Greaves, find Jenkins. And use any means necessary to stop him,' said Cuthbertson.

'Right away, sir.'

Cuthbertson turned to a tall, bald-headed commando and looked him straight in the eye. The commando stood to attention.

'Captain Ayres, use your men to secure every possible entry point to the armoury. When you find Jenkins, try to take him alive. If all else fails, you are authorised to use lethal force.'

'Yes, sir.'

'Good luck.'

Ayres saluted and hurried away to organise his men.

'And what about the rest of the building?' said Quark. 'What about my laboratories?'

'Good point, Professor.'

'Control, order all agents to report for security duties.'

'I'll send the order out right away, sir,' said the Duty Officer.

****

Rusham led Clavity to Skyraptor-one's medical bay and encouraged him to lie down on a stretcher. It was a narrow space, but it was well equipped. A medic arrived and examined Clavity's wound. Commandos buzzed excitedly around the cargo deck and inspected their equipment. There had been several injuries during the recent aerobatics, and Rusham nodded in sympathy as men rubbed sore knees and elbows.

Sean enjoyed being on the flight deck because so much was happening. Scopes bleeped, and hundreds of lights blinked. Amidst constant chatter, the crew prepared for their mission. He discovered that Skyraptor-two was codenamed Deuce, and was going to join them on their mission. The plan was to find Krankhausen's base and send in an assault team.

'Deuce, this is Sunbeam, join us on our starboard side,' said Reynard.

'Will do, Sunbeam. Our ETA is two minutes.'

'Flight, take us above the clouds,' said Reynard. 'Radar, any sign of drones?'

'Nothing on our scanners, sir.'

'Keep looking. They may be more out there.'

A few minutes later, heads turned to watch a flickering shape outside.

'Sunbeam, this is Deuce; we are alongside you now.'

Through a cockpit window, Sean spotted the faint outline

of an aircraft flying beside them. It was long and slender with four swept wings and twin angular tailfins. The aircraft looked beautiful and menacing at the same time.

'Deuce, prepare for a video link,' said Reynard, adjusting his camera.

'This is Deuce, go ahead.'

Reynard raised a hand in greeting. Sean strained to see a tiny blonde head appear on Reynard's personal screen.

'Lieutenant, glad you could join us,' said Reynard.

'I wouldn't miss it for the world, sir.'

'We don't know what Krankhausen has in store for us down there, so we're going to play it safe. As much as it pains me, we need to take him alive.'

'Understood, Captain.'

'Prepare for a steep pass and stay close. We'll use aerial mines to smoke him out, and we'll re-group for the main event. Any questions?'

'No, sir. We're raring to go.'

'Good luck, Lieutenant.'

'Good luck to you, sir.'

****

Krankhausen ushered Greerbo to a large, blue screen. It showed two red shapes approaching the centre of a rectangular grid. The shapes flashed every time the scope swept over them.

'How did they find us, Greerbo? We should be invisible to their sensors.'

'I don't know, boss.'

'Shoot them down! I don't care how. Throw everything we have at them!'

Greerbo eyed a nervous gathering of technicians.

'Yes, boss, it will be my pleasure. You heard the man, get to work!'

****

'Crew, this is Reynard. We've located Krankhausen's base, and we're about to begin our first pass. Strap yourselves in and prepare for a steep dive.'

In Skyraptor-one's hold, the commandos gave a loud cheer. Rusham and Clavity raised their eyebrows.

'Strange people these commandos,' whispered Clavity.

Rusham laughed.

'Stranger than your ex-colleagues in the Army?'

'I don't know what you mean,' said Clavity.

Sean watched heat shields slide over the cockpit windows, and the lights dimmed.

'Weapons, prepare smoke clusters and aerial mines,' said Reynard.

'All weapons are primed and ready to roll, sir.'

'Flight, take us in as fast as you can,' said Reynard.

'Commencing attack run in five, four, three, two, now.'

Sean felt his stomach tense and his ears pop. Skyraptor-one dived steeply and built up a tremendous speed. There was a loud rushing sound, and in seconds they were cutting through the clouds. They flew faster and faster, throwing Sean forwards against his straps, his cheeks rippling.

'Release mines when in range,' said Reynard.

'Mines away, sir.'

'Deuce confirms the release of their mines,' said Comms.

Skyraptor-one banked away into a steep climb. Behind them, a cluster of mines exploded in mid-air. It was louder than any firework display Sean had ever heard. However, the strain on his stomach made him cry out, and the seat dug into the small of his back. He closed his eyes and wished they could slow down.

'Three missiles tracking us have been shot down, sir,' said Weapons.

'Deuce, are you with us?' said Reynard

'Right on your tail, Sunbeam.'

'Head for the outer marker,' said Reynard.

'Will do, Sunbeam, out.'

****

Krankhausen struggled to his feet and looked up as a deep rumble of aircraft engines faded into the distance. The glass roof had splintered like a spider's web, yet somehow it held together. However, the sun and sky were blocked out by a dense fog, and not even the lower decks were visible.

'Did we hit them?' said Krankhausen to no one in particular.

No one replied because only a handful of technicians were left. The rest had escaped while they had the chance. Those who remained staggered back to their stations. Sparks fizzed from a row of computers, and Greerbo sprayed them with a fire extinguisher which only hastened their demise. Krankhausen seized a weapon from a fallen bodyguard and turned to his depleted crew. A guard recovered into a kneeling position and put his hands up in surrender, but Krankhausen ignored him.

'If anyone else is thinking of leaving, they'll have me to answer to!' he cried, waving the gun in the air.

The technicians froze.

'Get back to your stations!' cried Krankhausen.

'Now!' said Greerbo.

****

Sean began to relax as Skyraptor-one settled into a level cruise. After all the excitement, his body needed a rest. The shutters slid open, and he watched majestic clouds rise to meet them.

'Deuce, this is Sunbeam. What is your status?' said Reynard.

'We took some minor damage, but all our systems are operational.'

'Prepare for a low-level missile attack and follow us down,' said Reynard.

'Will do, Sunbeam, out.'

Sean braced himself for another dive, but this time they descended in a wide corkscrew, which seemed to go on forever.

'Radar, any signs of enemy activity?' said Reynard.

'No, sir, there's nothing on our scopes. I think we've knocked out their tracking systems.'

'We'll see,' said Reynard. 'Flight, begin your attack run.'

Sean watched the ocean become nearer and nearer. White flecks became waves, and the bluish-grey surface grew into an expanse of constantly moving water.

'We're going to land in the sea!'

'Relax, Sean, they're professionals,' said Rusham.

A grinding, mechanical sound rumbled beneath them.

'Main weapons bay open, sir.'

'Prepare to launch targeting drones on my command,' said Reynard '3, 2, 1, launch!'

Sean heard a sound like thunder, and a fiery missile emerged ahead of them. It cruised above the sea and was joined by an identical twin on a parallel course. The two craft accelerated away and vanished into the distance. A cloud of smoke hung on the horizon, and flashes of red light shone erratically in all directions.

'Flight, increase our altitude for weapons launch,' said Reynard.

Sean flinched as they rose once more.

'Weapons, launch Hammerheads and climb to observation height,' said Reynard.

A whining sound of hydraulic motors was followed by another loud roar. Skyraptor-one banked to the right and increased its height.

****

Krankhausen sensed the fog was beginning to lift and raised his binoculars. He noticed two grey dots in the distance. The platform's defences tried to lock onto them and fired laser beams into the sky, but every shot was wayward. Krankhausen realised the targeting system was damaged and cursed in frustration. The dots grew into tiny aircraft and flew ever closer. Gatling guns pounded the sky with lead, but the attackers divided and increased their speed.

'It'll take more than two missiles to scare me!'

For a split second, Krankhausen saw a flicker of a blue and grey aircraft in the distance. Two stubby cylinders fell from out of nowhere. They split apart and dropped countless needle-like shapes towards the sea. Every needle sprouted flames and began to race towards them. Krankhausen quivered.

'Greerbo! Lower the Orca! We're leaving!'

Chaos broke out on the main deck. The remaining guards and technicians ran for their lives. Krankhausen fired warning shots into the air but only succeeded in making them run faster. Moments later, the first missiles shook the platform like an earthquake. A laser turret exploded below them, followed by another and another. Overhead, the fragile roof shattered into millions of shards. Technicians and guards dived for cover wherever they could. Some took refuge under tables or equipment racks. Others ran for stairwells and went in search of life rafts on the lower decks.

Krankhausen tucked his head under his arms and ran for an exit pursued by Greerbo. They had almost reached the stairs when they were thrown off their feet by another wave of explosions. The platform lurched to one side, and the deck shook as numerous missiles reached their targets. Beneath them, girders groaned, and a whole section of the living quarters fell into the sea. Yet, somehow, the main deck remained intact. When it seemed the worst was over, a drilling tower high above them creaked. It fell with an almighty crash and flattened one side of the platform like cardboard. Greerbo helped Krankhausen to his feet, and together they limped to the stairs.

Skyraptor-one slowed to a crawl, and Sean spotted a column of black smoke streaming from a damaged structure in the distance. It resembled an elaborate oil rig and had concentric rings of rounded decks and turrets. One side had collapsed, and the twisted girders of a collapsed tower leaned at a sharp angle towards the sea.

'What's happening?'

Clavity peered out of the cockpit window and clenched his fist.

'We've got him!'

But Sean was distracted. A vision of swirling water filled his mind, and he slumped back in his seat.

'Sean, what's the matter?' said Reynard.

'Someone's coming.'

'Who?'

'I don't know. But they're angry, and they want revenge.'

Meanwhile, a murmur of happy voices filled the flight deck.

'Flight, prepare to recover our targeting drone,' said Reynard.

'Slowing to hover speed, sir.'

'Targeting drone is on course, ETA two minutes,' said Weapons.

'Deuce, prepare your assault teams for deployment,' said Reynard.

'Will do, Sunbeam. We are recovering our targeting drone and will deploy shortly.'

****

Jenkins thumped a vent cover until it swung open on its hinges. He craned his neck to scan the room below and was relieved to find it empty. He crawled forwards, squeezed his hips through the opening, and dropped to the floor with a thump. His bare feet landed heavily on a hard floor, but he felt almost nothing. Nor did he notice a fresh cut on his stomach. Jenkins crouched and looked around. The office contained a desk, a chair, and a bookshelf but little else. There was an outside window and a glass panel beside an interior door. In many respects, it was similar to his own office. In fact, he remembered visiting the room for meetings. But that was before Cuthbertson had betrayed him; and before his sister had been attacked in her own home. He snarled at the memories.

Jenkins realised he was only three floors above the armoury. All he needed was to gain access to a secure lift at the far end of the corridor. He scoured the room for weapons and tools, but all he could find were pieces of furniture and a metal coat stand. He decided to improvise.

Visions of fire and destruction filled his troubled mind. When would they leave him in peace? Jenkins remembered his poor twin sister and vowed Cuthbertson would pay a dear price for what he had done to her.

CHAPTER 12: DESCENT

Clavity felt restless. The medic had stitched up his cut, and his forehead was covered in bandages. His hair stood up like a brush, but he felt much better.

'Look at you, you hero,' said Rusham.

'For crashing into a chair? Still, I'd rather be a hero than an accident-prone old man,' said Clavity. 'What do you think Reynard's up to now? We can't have him running off after Krankhausen on his own, now can we?'

'I think they're preparing for an assault,' said Rusham.

Clavity frowned. It would be typical of Reynard to take all the glory. According to the rumour mill, it was how he had won his promotion in the first place.

'I'm going to check on Sean. Don't go anywhere, Major.'

Clavity rattled his stretcher in protest. However, he was pinned down by a blanket and straps.

'I don't suppose you could...'

Rusham watched him wriggle about and smiled.

'And spoil your bed rest, Major? Not a chance. You heard the medic.'

Rusham stepped out into the corridor and was almost knocked over.

'Watch out, love! Coming through!'

She sidestepped two burly commandos who wheeled a long, black missile towards the front of the aircraft. They wore full body armour and what appeared to be glide suits. Across their shoulders, they carried weapons she had not seen before. Rusham winced as the commandos bulldozed their way past. She heard two more approaching and hurried upstairs before they arrived. A speaker on the wall came alive.

'This is Reynard. Assault Teams prepare for deployment in ten minutes.'

Rusham gave a wry smile. Clavity would be annoyed to

miss the action.

Skyraptor-one turned to face Krankhausen's base.
Determined to watch the assault, Sean undid his seat belt and
moved to get a better view. He watched the platform
smoulder, but something was different. Sean studied a screen
hanging from the ceiling to find out what it was. They
approached the platform like a cat stalking a mouse. Ahead of
them, Deuce glinted before its camouflage adjusted, and it
blended back into its surroundings.

'Enjoying the view?' said Reynard.

'Err, yes,' said Sean, taken aback. 'But what's that hanging
from Krankhausen's base?'

Suspended beneath the platform was a torpedo-shaped
object, which appeared to be moving towards the sea.
Reynard moved a joystick on his command console and
zoomed in for a closer look.

'He's trying to escape! Well spotted, Sean.'

'Weapons, I need a precise laser strike,' said Reynard.

'Where, sir?'

'Your target is on the main screen now.'

The image zoomed in to show a small, grey submarine
being lowered by four cables. It was elliptical in shape, with
fins fore and aft.

'Aim for the winching gear,' said Reynard, highlighting a
mechanism on the screen.

'Powering up the laser now.'

'Fire when ready,' said Reynard.

Sean watched the winch glow yellow and white. It sparked
as the metal deformed and gave way. The submarine juddered
and came to a halt.

'Pierce the sub as well,' said Reynard.

There was a sudden flash of red light from the platform,
and Skyraptor-two appeared in full view. It was damaged on
its near-side, and smoke poured from a burning gash in its
hull. Behind its wings, horizontal fans span in a hazy blur. At
its tail, two engines pounded the waves in wide circles of

exhaust fumes.

'Sunbeam, this is Deuce. We are taking incoming fire.'

'Do you need to withdraw?' said Reynard.

'Negative, Sunbeam, we have contained the damage. We are about to deploy our assault teams. Can you provide covering fire?'

'Will do, Deuce. Weapons, locate the incoming laser and destroy it.'

'Yes, sir.'

Two more laser beams struck Krankhausen's base, and the submarine lurched downwards on one side. A coupling gave way, and a cable fell into the sea. Another laser cut into the submarine's hull, which promptly caught fire. Meanwhile, a small dome on the platform exploded.

'We have disabled the hostile's laser, sir.'

'Excellent. Flight, take us in for a closer look,' said Reynard.

Sean watched three flattened missiles emerge from the mouth of Skyraptor-two. As they hovered past, he realised the missiles had double V-shaped wings and figures hunched behind raised fairings. The strange craft threw out jets of flame and accelerated towards Krankhausen's base.

****

Greerbo staggered onto the viewing deck, weighed down by a cache of weapons. Dangling from his arms and shoulders, he carried a missile launcher, a machine gun, and a portable laser. He dropped them with a loud clank on the metal walkway. Krankhausen strode ahead of him and marched up to some railings. He raised his binoculars and studied the sky through infra-red filters.

'Hurry up! I've spotted them!'

Greerbo gazed at the pile of weapons on the deck.

'Launch the missile!' said Krankhausen.

Greerbo picked up a long tube and pointed it at the empty sky.

'But what am I firing at, boss?'

'Straight ahead,' said Krankhausen, indicating at a patch of cloud in the distance.

'Where?'

Krankhausen let out a snarl.

'Just fire, will you?'

Greerbo unleashed the missile. It spiralled through the air, unguided, before splashing into the sea wide of its intended target.

'Useless!' said Krankhausen.

'But, boss…'

'Don't *boss* me!'

Tiny aircraft appeared out of nowhere, flying low above the sea. Through his binoculars, Krankhausen spotted a Foundation aircraft. It hovered with its loading ramp extended. He watched commandos emerge and realised they would arrive within minutes. He started to panic.

'Give me the laser!' he said, snatching it from Greerbo. 'And fetch the Matteract! Hurry!'

'Yes, boss,' said Greerbo.

Krankhausen steadied himself against the railing. He used one hand to hold the laser and the other to focus the binoculars. It was not an easy task. Satisfied with his aim, Krankhausen squeezed the fire button and held it down. The laser unleashed a burst of light and struck home.

'Yes!' he cried.

A small patch on one side of the Foundation aircraft began to smoke. Krankhausen tried to fire again. This time the laser beeped, but nothing happened.

'Pathetic weapon!' he said and hurled the spent weapon onto the deck. Where were his beautiful drones when he needed them?

Greerbo returned carrying a grey fluted tube attached to a cylinder and a trigger assembly. A series of pipes encircled its barrel, and a trailing lead connected the device to a power pack. Krankhausen licked his lips.

'Help me set it up, Greerbo,' he said, taking hold of the

lighter end of the weapon.

Greerbo grunted and dragged the power pack behind him.

'When is it my turn, boss?'

'When I say so.'

By now, the first commandos were in range. Krankhausen ignored them and aimed at the damaged Skyraptor hovering in full view. The Matteract whined for a moment before releasing its deadly rays. A burst of invisible particles sped across the water and boiled a corridor of seawater. It swept past two miniature aircraft and struck the Skyraptor on one of its wings.

'Gotcha!' said Krankhausen.

Greerbo cheered and shook his fist. The damaged Skyraptor span and ducked wildly in the air. Krankhausen felt sure it would only be a matter of time until it crashed into the sea. He fired again, but the Matteract was dead. At that precise moment, Krankhausen realised the battle was over. What few weapons they had left would only delay the inevitable, and now his mini-submarine was crippled.

'It was good though, wasn't it?' he said, flushed with triumph at hitting the Skyraptor.

'Yes, boss. But remember, we still have the drone ships!'

'Then what are we waiting for?' said Krankhausen, grinning.

They turned to leave but could not resist a chuckle at the stricken Skyraptor.

****

'Mayday! Mayday! This is Deuce. We're going down!'

Skyraptor-two wheeled around, and its pilot battled for control. Sean noticed half a wing had vanished in a burst of heat and steam. Its trailing pair had also been damaged and hung limp, offering no lift. Behind it, the remains of an engine spewed out smoke and pieces of shrapnel. The Skyraptor veered and dipped towards the sea. It balanced on its two remaining engines and lurched sideways before being corrected by its pilot.

'Abandon ship! Abandon ship! Deploy all commandos and support crew.'

Reynard was in shock. His first instinct was to destroy Krankhausen's base in revenge. However, he hastily reconsidered. The entire mission depended on his next decision, and he knew it.

'Weapons, fire stun grenades at those two jokers.'

Soon the commandos would reach Krankhausen. Soon their mission would be over. It would be men against boys or, in this case, highly equipped rhinos against a short, stocky man and a pasty-faced stick insect.

'Grenades away, sir.'

Reynard glanced at the main screen and watched the projectiles arc towards Krankhausen's base. The subsequent events unfolded in painful slow-motion. The first grenade hit a railing and exploded some distance from the two figures. It was followed by a second, which bounced and hit the stocky man full in the chest, knocking him over. The grenade rolled away and exploded on the deck, sending both men sprawling.

'Was that our suspect, Captain?' said Rusham, returning to the flight deck.

'What's left of him,' said Reynard.

'Any chance of someone picking up the pieces?'

'Our first assault team will be there any second.'

The stocky man lay flat on his back, his head dangling over the sea, but there was no sign of Krankhausen.

'Better start looking in the water then.'

Reynard blanched and tapped his earpiece to relay the orders.

Sean stepped forwards and pointed at Krankhausen's platform.

'They've arrived,' he said in a calm voice.

'Who have, Sean? The commandos?' said Rusham.

Sean closed his eyes, and a vision of swirling water filled his mind.

'The others. They're here.'

'Sunbeam, this is Deuce. Our engines can't hold much longer. We're preparing to ditch. Anything that floats would be useful right now.'

'Deuce, we're coming to assist,' said Reynard. 'Briggs, prepare to launch our life rafts.'

Sean's legs gave way. He felt Rusham catch him before he fell to the floor.

'What's the matter with him?' said Reynard.

'I think he's fainted,' said Rusham.

But Sean was wide awake. In his mind, he stared into three cold, black eyes.

****

Jenkins crept across the office floor on his hands and knees. He heard footsteps in the corridor and watched shadows pass the office window. From their shapes and sounds, he realised they were commandos. They were most likely heading towards the armoury lift.

'You won't find me out there,' he whispered.

Jenkins tried the door handle. It was locked. He tiptoed to the desk and rifled through its top drawer. Sure enough, on a plastic tray, he found a spare door key and a lighter.

'Tut-tut,' he said and took both.

Jenkins returned to the door and tested the key. He heard the lock clunk and turn. Satisfied there was no one approaching, he dropped to his hands and knees and opened the door a few inches. The corridor looked much as Jenkins remembered, and it was deserted. However, a sudden noise on his left made him jump. Footsteps rang out, and a communicator crackled into life. It was a commando making his report.

Jenkins crept back into the office and closed the door. He waited for the commando's footsteps to fade and sprang into action. He wheeled a pedestal out from under the desk and parked it next to the door. Next, he dragged the coat stand across the room and mounted it lengthways on top of the pedestal. Finally, he prised a small whiteboard from a wall and propped it up behind the base of the coat stand. With some difficulty, Jenkins pushed his shaky contraption out into the corridor and turned left, zigzagging as he went.

Two commandos appeared from around a corner. At once, Jenkins realised he had to act. They paused for a second, bemused by the sight in front of them, and Jenkins charged. He was quick but not quick enough. The first commando raised his rifle and fired a neat pattern of holes through the whiteboard. The bullets flew over Jenkins' head and missed him by a whisker.

'Play nicely, gents!' he cried and rammed the front of the coat stand into the first commando's groin.

The commando howled and grabbed his colleague, pulling him off-balance, which gave Jenkins a few vital seconds. He sprinted past them and around the corner. Gunfire sounded, and a bullet clipped the top of his shoulder. But Jenkins was gone. He dived headfirst into a waste disposal chute and slid to the basement. As he tumbled into darkness, Jenkins felt a rush of adrenalin and a harsh sting in his shoulder.

'Soon, it will be your turn to feel pain,' he muttered.

CHAPTER 13: OLD SCHOOL

Lieutenant Marsh paced the length of Skyraptor-two and checked his crew had evacuated. He secured the bulkhead doors and activated the Skyraptor's floatation devices. Compressors roared and filled the inside of the aircraft with inflated helium cushions. Marsh realised he was fortunate to have this opportunity. If Krankhausen had been a better shot, they would already be at the bottom of the ocean. Or worse, they would be vapour. He reached the flight deck and found the pilot and co-pilot struggling with the controls.

'We can't hold her much longer, sir,' said the pilot.

'Okay, let's do it. Ditch all our weapons,' said Marsh.

'Weapons released, sir,' said the co-pilot in a deadpan voice.

Beneath them, missiles, torpedoes, and mines plunged into the sea, but not a single one exploded.

'Weapons bay empty and sealed, sir.'

'Good, when you're ready, gentlemen.'

The pilot and co-pilot hurried through an on-screen checklist.

'We need breathing masks, sir,' said the pilot.

'I'll fetch them,' said Marsh.

He raised a floor panel marked in red and hauled out two bags of emergency equipment. They contained survival kits, lifejackets, an inflatable boat, and portable breathing masks.

'Shame you don't have a spare wing in there,' said the pilot.

In theory, Skyraptors were designed to float for several hours, but that was with a complete set of wings. To make matters worse, the pilots had to seal up the rear engine compartments and land with only one hover motor to slow their descent.

'Here,' said Marsh, brandishing a pair of masks.

He helped the pilot and co-pilot to pull them over their

faces and strapped himself into a seat.

'Make it a good one, Flight.'

'Will do, sir.'

Marsh attached his own mask, and the pilot began the countdown.

'Three, two, one, now.'

The rear engines cut out, and the aircraft lurched downwards. By keeping the remaining engine on full throttle, they slowed a little before veering to their right and plunging into the sea.

On impact, all three men were thrown forwards. Marsh watched seawater dim the cockpit and emergency lights came on. It was an eerie sight.

'If we had to eject now, could we?'

'I doubt it, sir,' said the pilot. 'To my knowledge, it's never been attempted underwater.'

'We'd have to use the escape hatch and float to the surface,' said the co-pilot.

The Skyraptor sank for a few moments before slowly rising. It stayed low in the water and tipped sideways towards its intact wings.

Reynard watched with a heavy heart.

'Captain, two surface vessels are approaching from the west,' said Radar.

'Show me their positions.'

'On screen now, sir. They'll be in range in ten minutes.'

It was too soon for rescue craft, and in any case, the recovery teams would arrive from the northeast.

'Perhaps no one's told Krankhausen he's lost?' said Rusham.

'Either way, we have to protect Deuce and her crew,' said Reynard.

'Flight, let's take a closer look.'

'Yes, sir.'

Sean woke from his trance and gazed around the flight deck. He found Rusham beside him.

'How are you feeling?'

'We need to save the commandos.'

'Save them from who?'

'From them,' said Sean, pointing at the smoking platform.

'Commandos are as tough as nails, Sean. They can look after themselves.'

Two commandos, Chan and Stevens, flew on a level course towards Krankhausen's base. They had rehearsed their attack plan at least a dozen times in virtual reality but this was different. Behind them, two more teams followed on either side. Chan needed to get it right, and he knew it. His first goal was to find a safe landing site. Given the state of the charred platform, that would not be easy.

'I'm going to fly past and take a closer look.'

'Copy that,' said Stevens.

Their TAC, or Two-person Attack Craft, raced a few feet above the sea at over eighty knots. It was lightweight and agile but had a limited range. To be effective, Chan and Stevens needed to work as a team which took months of training.

'How's our fuel burn?' said Chan.

'Fine, provided we land soon.'

'Okay, I'm going to buzz the main dome. Get ready to return fire.'

'Locked and loaded,' said Stevens, priming his weapon.

Chan slowed to seventy knots and steered the TAC into a shallow climb. Behind him, Stevens steadied his weapon.

'We'll reach the target in thirty seconds.'

The sea ahead of them began to bubble furiously, and a ring of foam became visible around Krankhausen's base. Chan thought nothing of it and continued his approach.

'What's happening down there?' said Stevens, preparing the weapon.

A giant waterspout rose from the sea. It spiralled upwards at an alarming rate and surrounded Krankhausen's base like a seething wall.

'Hold on!' cried Chan, accelerating into a steep turn

The thundering water stretched outwards until it surrounded the entire platform like a funnel. Chan tried to turn away, but they were already too close. Their TAC hit the waterspout head-on and was carried upwards. The vortex snapped their safety tethers and threw them both into the sea like rag dolls.

****

In the basement at Foundation HQ, Jenkins rubbed his sore limbs. He had landed in a heap on a bare concrete floor and ached all over. His shoulder burned, and his knees began to bleed.

'Typical!' he said, cursing the lack of rubbish to cushion his fall.

Jenkins sat in a large barren space. It contained a compactor and furnace on one side and a heating system on the other. Apart from the constant hum of an air conditioning unit, everything was quiet. He considered a row of metal cupboards. From memory, he knew they housed circuit breakers and meters, but Jenkins was looking for something far more interesting. He turned his attention to the heating system.

Jenkins' mind raced with scenes of a house under attack. Foundation commandos unleashed a barrage of gunfire. Windows shattered, and brickwork was damaged in the onslaught. His sister cowered beside a bedroom cupboard while bullet holes peppered the walls around her. One of the commandos fired a smoke grenade. It crashed through a bedroom window and set light to the curtains. As the flames began to spread, Jenkins felt a rage grow inside him. How could Cuthbertson live with himself after what he'd done? The Foundation was supposed to protect their own.

He limped over to the heating system and sought out its control box. He found it mounted on a wall, several feet from the burner. It had a metal cover secured by a twisted wire and a plastic tag. Jenkins sighed in disgust and stretched the seal apart using his screwdriver. On his second attempt, it gave way, and he tore open the cover. Jenkins switched off the gas burner and was greeted by stillness. Now the fun could begin. He set to work uncoupling pipes from the heating system and opening valves. The unmistakable smell of gas wafted under his nose, and Jenkins hurried away in search of an exit.

****

Skyraptor-one flew high above the sea and scanned the horizon. Two hydrofoils appeared on its radar screen, heading towards them at a tremendous speed.

'Radar, do you have a lock?' said Reynard.

'No, sir, I can't get a fix. Something's jamming our signals.'

'Not again?' said Reynard. 'How are they doing this?'

'They must know our technology, sir,' said Radar.

Reynard sighed.

'Is there any chance they're friendly?'

'I've tried signalling them on all international frequencies, sir,' said Comms. 'They're not replying.'

Sean was overcome with frustration. He rose from his seat and confronted Reynard.

'Can't you see?' They're *here*. *They're* doing this!'

'Enough of this nonsense!' said Reynard. 'We have serious work to do. Agent Rusham, please restrain this child!'

Rusham stepped forwards and reached for Sean's arm.

'Don't touch me!' said Sean, breaking free.

'It's okay,' said Rusham. 'I'll look after you.'

Sean allowed himself to be led back to his seat.

'Why doesn't anyone ever listen to me?'

Rusham gave a half-smile.

'I'm listening, Sean. What can you tell me?'

'It's all a blur,' said Sean. 'But I know something evil is out there watching us. It wants to destroy us.'

Reynard rolled his eyes and turned back to the main screen.

'We need to disable those hydrofoils and quickly. Does anyone have any ideas?'

'We could guide our missiles by sight,' said Weapons.

'Yeah, but they won't be guided,' said Flight.

'And what if they're shot down?' said Reynard. 'The hydrofoils are bound to have defences.'

The crew watched the radar as the hydrofoils sped towards them in a battle formation. Reynard zoomed in on their angular shapes.

'Or we could EMP the whole area,' said Weapons.

'With a Skyraptor and commandos in the water?' said Reynard. 'Come on, guys, we must have some better options?'

The flight deck fell silent for a moment.

'Why don't you try what they did in the Second World War?' said Sean.

'Meaning?' said Reynard.

'Submarines used to launch a fan of torpedoes at a convoy.'

Reynard looked dubious.

'It would at least force them to change course, sir,' said Weapons.

'It might slow them down, but how do we stop their attack?' said Reynard.

'We could launch *our* TACs?' said Flight. 'They should be able to cause some damage?'

'Good thinking!' said Reynard. 'And the torpedoes will buy us some time.'

'Weapons, prepare to target the nearest hydrofoil with a spread of three torpedoes.'

'Right away, sir.'

Reynard switched on the ship's intercom.

'Sergeant Briggs, prepare to deploy Assault Teams One, Two, and Three.'

'Briggs here, sir. What are their orders?'

'Two hydrofoils are approaching from the west. We need them disabled. Repeat, disable the hydrofoils.'

There was a crackle and a muffled sound of orders being relayed.

'Confirmed, Captain. The Assault Teams will scramble and engage.'

'Good luck, men. We're counting on you,' said Reynard.

'Torpedoes away, sir,' said Weapons.

'What do we have left?'

'One torpedo and six missiles.'

Reynard considered the situation. They had enough munitions to ward off the hydrofoils but not enough to guarantee victory.

'Flight, hold us steady. We need to protect our men in the water. Weapons, prepare the lasers and cannon.'

'Will do, sir.'

'Captain, you need to hear this,' said Comms.

'Patch them through,' said Reynard.

'Sunbeam, this is Deuce, over.'

'Go ahead, Deuce.'

'We've ditched, but we're still floating.'

'Good work, Lieutenant. The recovery teams will be here soon.'

'The trouble is we're being pulled towards a huge waterspout.'

'Say again?' said Reynard, not believing his ears.

'On screen now, sir,' said Radar.

'Mon Dieu!' said Reynard. 'What in the world is that?'

The main screen showed an enormous wall of swirling water surrounding Krankhausen's base. The platform itself was almost hidden.

****

Content with his work, Jenkins staggered to the bottom of a lift shaft. He found a small maintenance hatch and turned two levers to release its cover. The levers creaked but did not release the hatch.

'Come on!'

Enraged, Jenkins sat down and pounded the hatch with the soles of his feet. The punishment was relentless, and his feet began to bleed. After numerous impacts, the concrete casing cracked, and the hatch fell inwards.

'Hey! Who's there?' cried a voice from above.

'Your worst nightmare,' whispered Jenkins, crawling into the shaft.

He balanced on a ledge and felt his way in the dark. Meanwhile, lasers flickered back and forth searching for a target. Jenkins felt along the wall and found a piece of cold metal jutting out from the concrete. It was the escape ladder. He grinned and reached into the waistband of his shorts. The lighter was still there. From the open hatch came a pungent smell of gas. Jenkins began to climb.

'Halt!' cried a voice.

Two shots ricocheted off the walls, and Jenkins laughed to himself.

'Is that the best you can do?'

As he climbed, Jenkins realised he was in the wrong lift shaft. The armoury was deep underground, but the ladder only led upwards.

'There's more than one way to punish a traitor,' he mused.

CHAPTER 14: DRASTIC ACTION

Sean followed Agent Rusham to the medical bay. He was still annoyed with Reynard for ignoring his warnings, but at least his torpedo idea had been put into practice.

'Let's see how grumpy-drawers is doing,' said Rusham.

Clavity grunted and opened his eyes. He was lying on a narrow stretcher attached to the wall.

'Hi, Major,' said Sean, in a deflated voice.

'What's wrong? I thought we were winning?'

'It's getting weird out there,' said Rusham.

'And *they've* arrived,' said Sean.

'Who's arrived? The recovery teams?'

Sean noticed Clavity struggle to free himself and knelt to loosen the straps on his bed. Clavity sat up, despite Rusham's disapproving glare.

'I can feel something evil out there, and it's taken Krankhausen.'

'*What?*' said Clavity.

'No one can see anything because of that waterspout,' said Rusham. 'And hydrofoils are preparing to attack.'

'Waterspout? Hydrofoils?' said Clavity. 'And what's Reynard doing about this?'

'Panicking mostly,' said Rusham.

Clavity flushed.

'And you think someone's turned up to rescue Krankhausen?'

'I'm sure of it,' said Sean.

Clavity gave Rusham a look of thunder.

'But there's no way through it, Major. The waterspout's surrounded Krankhausen's base.'

'Can't we go over it or under it?' said Clavity.

'Have you seen how powerful that thing is?' said Rusham.

Sean laughed at the squabbling agents.

'And I suppose *you* have a better idea?' said Clavity.

Sean was taken aback for a moment. He spread his hands wide and gave a weak grin.

'Couldn't we make a hole in it?'

'Are you joking?' said Rusham. 'It's enormous! And it's already wiped out our best commandos.'

'Hold that thought,' said Clavity, raising a hand to calm things. 'What if we *could* punch a hole through this waterspout?'

'Like Krankhausen did when he broke into my bedroom,' said Sean, his eyes ablaze.

Clavity smiled.

'You're a genius!'

'I don't understand,' said Rusham.

'How many TACs do we have on board?'

Rusham pursed her lips.

'About five, I guess.'

'And what's mounted on a TAC?' said Clavity.

'Whatever you like. A machine gun, a laser, or a grenade launcher.'

'What about a Matteract?'

'You can't be serious?' said Rusham, pulling a face.

Clavity gave a nod.

'But who's going to fly it?' said Rusham, staring at Clavity's bandages.

'Do you think Reynard will lend us any of his commandos?' said Clavity.

'Not a chance.'

'Which means Krankhausen's going to get away.'

Rusham let out a sigh.

'Alright, I'll do it. But I'll need someone to fire the Matteract.'

'I'll go!' said Sean.

Rusham and Clavity eyed each other.

'We can't, can we?'

'Who else can we trust?' said Clavity.

'But what about the Brigadier?'

'How good is your flying?'

****

Agent Lee felt her watch buzz and read an incoming message: *The Foundation is on red alert. All agents must return to HQ immediately. Report to Security on arrival.*

'Hmm, looks like the party's over.'

She considered how best to manage the situation. Her team would need to pack the van and bring Mrs Yeager with them, which would be fun. She was still climbing the walls after her son's disappearance. Well, what was left of her walls. Lee had tried to reassure her that Sean was in safe hands. However, Mrs Yeager had launched into a full-blown rant for at least twenty minutes. Lee went in search of her second-in-command.

'We could always tell her we're going to collect her son?' said Brown.

'Sure, and you can explain why Sean's not at HQ when we get there.'

Brown gave a pained expression.

'Needs must.'

'You said it. Right, let's load up and ship out.'

****

Professor Quark followed Ayres down a fire escape staircase. Ahead of them, three commandos scanned the stairwell through laser sights.

'How long has Jenkins been in there?' said Quark.

'I don't know, Professor. Ten, maybe twenty minutes? He tried to escape in a life shaft, but we have him penned in.'

'I heard he floored one of your men?'

'Two,' said Ayres. 'He's a wild animal.'

'But he's only slight,' said Quark.

'It took three men to restrain him.'

'And yet he escaped?'

'Indeed,' said Ayres. 'I've never seen anything like it.'

At the bottom of the staircase, they reached a fire door. It was locked. The commandos looked to their leader for guidance.

'Best stand bank, Professor,' said Ayres, skipping down the last few steps. 'Alright, lads, we'll have to blow it off its hinges.'

****

Rusham led Sean to the forward loading ramp. The cargo bay was empty except for two TACs which sat on their cradles. One was flight-ready and positioned facing the open ramp. Rusham tried to remember the last time she had flown one, years ago. A strong breeze ruffled her hair.

'Can I help you?' said a voice.

Rusham froze and squinted in the daylight. A man dressed in camouflage stood beside the ramp controls. He was as wide as he was tall, and Rusham quickly realised he was a Sergeant.

'Well?' said Briggs.

'Captain Reynard wants to see you on the flight deck,' said Rusham, putting on her brightest smile.

Briggs considered this and rubbed his neck.

'Then why didn't he call me on the intercom?'

'He says it's a private matter,' said Rusham, trying to sound convincing.

Briggs glared at her.

'Right then, jump to it!' he said, marching towards the rear of the cargo bay. 'We can't keep the Captain waiting now, can we?'

Rusham winked at Sean.

'Captain Reynard told us to stay in the medical bay.'

'Quite right too,' said Briggs. 'Carry on.'

Briggs reached the metal staircase and began to climb to the flight deck. As he did so, Rusham pulled Sean to one side.

'Let's go,' she whispered and ushered him back to the ramp.

114

Rusham untied the TAC's restraints as quickly as she could and searched a locker for flight gear.

'Here, put these on,' she said, thrusting a helmet and life vest into Sean's arms.

Sean put on the life vest. It smothered his narrow frame, but he did his best to tighten its straps. The helmet was a better fit, and Sean fastened it under his chin.

'You clip yourself on here,' said Rusham, pointing at a metal D-ring on the TAC.

'Huh?' said Sean.

Rusham clipped and unclipped the tether on her life vest to demonstrate. She adjusted his life vest and checked his helmet.

'Right, got it,' said Sean, clambering onto his seat.

'And hold on tight. You'll find handles and footrests on either side.'

Sean felt a tingling in his stomach. He attached his tether and rested his sneakers on the footrests. It was a streamlined machine, and the prospect of flying made him tremble with excitement. Rusham returned carrying a weapon, which she clamped on a mounting in front of him. She adjusted its barrel and slid it sideways before tightening some levers. Rusham climbed onto the pilot's seat and put on her helmet.

'See if you can reach the trigger, but don't touch it,' she said over the intercom.

Sean discovered he could only reach the trigger if he released his tether. It was a small detail that he decided to keep to himself.

'Yes, I can,' he said, re-attaching himself.

Rusham switched on the TAC and flicked through its controls in a hurry.

'Whatever you do, don't fire until I tell you. Seriously, Sean, that Matteract could melt a ship in seconds. We'll only have one chance.'

'Got it,' said Sean.

He peered over Rusham's shoulder at the expanse of ocean and began to have second thoughts. What if they crashed or were shot down?

'Hey! What are you doing?' cried a voice behind them.

It was Briggs.

'Get off there this instant! That's commando property!'

'Hold on!' said Rusham.

Sean's heart skipped a beat, and his adrenalin kicked in. Briggs ran towards them, waving his fist as Rusham lit up the TAC's engines. She gunned its throttle and sent them hurtling out of the cargo bay. Sean gripped the TAC for all he was worth and was flung backwards. He managed to stay onboard thanks to his safety harness and their sudden plunge towards the sea.

Reynard waited for news from his assault teams and watched the hydrofoils close in. They avoided the torpedoes with ease. On the main screen, he identified several missile canisters on their decks.

'Our sensors are still out of action, sir,' said Radar.

'Flight, prepare to withdraw,' said Reynard.

From beneath them came the sudden roar of a jet engine.

'What was that?' said the pilot, straining to peer over his controls.

'Rusham!' said Reynard in a fury.

'Our loading bay door is jammed open, sir. It's not responding,' said Weapons.

'And our flight controls, sir. We're stuck in hover-mode.'

Reynard tried to take it all in. Jammed controls, approaching missile ships, and a disobedient agent were all he needed. His left eyelid began to twitch.

'Look!' said Weapons, pointing at the main screen.

The nearest hydrofoil began to rotate a missile launcher towards them. The crew watched in horror as it tilted the canister skyward.

'Do we have *any* weapons operational?' said Reynard.

'Only short-range cannon, sir.'

'Weapons, come with me,' said Reynard, leaping out of his chair. 'I have an idea!'

CHAPTER 15: SPARKS

Professor Quark received urgent news from his team. He tried to phone Cuthbertson, but his calls went straight to voicemail. In frustration, he left a message.

'What's the point of a mobile phone if no one answers it?' he grumbled to himself.

His team had at last restored the computer system. The original computers were now only fit for the scrap heap. Jenkins' viruses had ravaged their programs and hard drives in seconds, leaving only burnt-out circuit boards. However, despite the budget cuts, Quark's team had tucked away some old computers. He considered presenting Cuthbertson with a bill for repairs when the emergency was over.

Quark had asked his team to review Jenkins' files in more detail. They discovered someone had gone to great lengths to forge Jenkins' records stretching back many years. The changes were so well executed, it was now difficult to distinguish truth from fiction. He also asked his team to check Jenkins' details against secret Government and Police records. As expected, they pieced together a consistent picture about Jenkins and his parents. However, there was not a single mention of his sister. Nor was there a birth certificate, school registration, or medical records. It was as if Jenkins' sister had never existed. Someone had invented her.

Quark's nose twitched, and he turned his attention to the basement. A familiar caustic smell irritated his nose.

'Stop! I can smell gas!' he cried.

Ayres waved his men away from the fire door, and they reluctantly lowered their weapons.

'I can't smell anything, Professor,' said Ayres, inside his combat helmet and facemask.

The commandos looked to Quark for an explanation.

'Stand back,' he said, pulling a small silver device from his jacket pocket.

Quark swept it around the stairwell and approached the fire door. Huffing and puffing, the commandos shuffled out of his way. Although the fire door was sealed tight, Quark's sensor beeped. An orange symbol flashed on its screen and turned red as he approached the door.

'Methane,' said Quark. 'It seems our friend Jenkins has been meddling with the gas supply.'

'I knew he was up to something,' said Ayres. 'What should we do?'

Quark paused for thought.

'First, we need to cut off the gas supply. Then we need to pump the basement full of flame retardant.'

'Come on, team. You heard the Professor,' said Ayres, leading his men upstairs.

****

Jenkins continued his climb in total darkness. It was hard work, and although his body was full of adrenalin, he began to tire. Laser sights scanned the lift shaft, but the voices were now below him. He chuckled to himself. It had been so easy to slip past the guards. The fools had assumed they could use the lift car to block his path. Little did they realise, he had squeezed by in the crevice where the service ladder was mounted. He paused for a moment and felt vibrations in the ladder. Someone was following him.

Jenkins bumped his head against something hard and unyielding. He reared back and almost fell. To his surprise, Jenkins had reached a concrete ceiling. On a lower rung, he fumbled in his waistband. The lighter was still there, and he sparked it into life. Its tiny flame revealed a shaft wall caked in dirt and oil. Above him was a concrete shelf and further up there was a set of winching gear. However, there was no sign of a maintenance hatch. Jenkins rubbed and scraped at the wall with his bare hands.

'Hold it right there!' cried a voice below.

Jenkins knew he was running out of time. He stepped

down a few rungs and continued to scrape at the wall. His fingernail caught something metallic. Could it be a hinge? Or a catch? He broke a nail but ignored the pain and continued to rub away layers of grime. Jenkins felt a metal seal in the wall and traced it with his fingers. Meanwhile, his left hand began to sting from the heat of the lighter. He ignored the pain and continued to search for an escape hatch.

'Crack!'

A shot grazed Jenkins' left wrist. He recoiled instinctively and let go of the lighter. It vanished into the gloom, and he braced himself. Jenkins heard it strike the shaft wall and clatter against the lift car, but there was no explosion. Jenkins cursed his bad luck and felt a wet trickle of blood ooze from his wrist.

'Ping!'

Another shot ricocheted past. This time it narrowly missed his head. Jenkins found a metal handle and turned it anti-clockwise. He gave it a hard shove, and a hatch door fell inward. It struck a commando full on his helmet, and Jenkins crawled through the opening. He landed head first on top of the unconscious commando and helped himself to his blaster and sidearm.

'Just what I was looking for,' he said with a grin.

****

Greaves was determined to make up for his earlier mistakes. Two of his best guards were in the medical wing, and he knew people were mocking him after Jenkins' escape. He equipped himself with a blaster, torch, and body armour. Jenkins had long since escaped to the basement, and Greaves followed his progress by listening to reports on his earpiece. He knew Ayres had sealed off the area and instructed everyone to await orders, but Greaves had other ideas.

'I'll get you, sonny boy,' he said, switching his blaster to full power. 'No one makes a fool out of me.'

Greaves jogged up a flight of stairs and followed in

Jenkins' footsteps. He found the first-floor corridor empty except for a plastic seal over a hole in the wall.

'A waste chute, how appropriate for trash like you,' he said.

Greaves cut the seal with a knife and stood back. Air rushed out as the pressure equalised. If his sense of smell had been keener, he would have stopped right there. Unfortunately, after a climbing accident, he could not even smell a clove of garlic under his nose. A fact that might also have explained the body odour problems he was reminded of almost every day. Greaves climbed into the waste chute feet first and sat on its outer edge. He steadied himself and took a deep breath, ready to confront Jenkins.

'Hey, you! Stop right there!' cried a voice behind him.

A commando sprinted down the corridor. Greaves let go and tried to slide away, but his armour snagged against the metal rim. He wriggled his hips to try and break free but found one of his wrists clamped in the commando's vice-like grip.

'Get your mutton hands off me!'

'Don't you get it? The basement's full of gas! One spark and the whole place will go up!'

Realising his mistake, Greaves tried to clamber out of the chute. However, as he wriggled his thighs, he caught a webbing clip against the edge of the chute. It pinged open, and his torch rolled along the edge of the chute before sliding downwards. Greaves swung his legs to try and catch it, but the torch slid past and was gone.

****

Lee and her team drove back to Foundation Headquarters through heavy traffic. Throughout the journey, Mrs Yeager gave the agents a tongue-lashing. In her view, they had destroyed her garden, killed her cat, poisoned her, kidnapped her son, and made her roof collapse. Her lawyers would be contacted, and everyone was sure to lose their jobs. All in all, it was turning out to be a most entertaining trip.

Mrs Yeager also threatened to jump from the van unless Sean was returned immediately. While Lee felt tempted to let her try, she realised she would be held responsible and activated the van's central locking. To compound matters, the medic refused to give Mrs Yeager any more treatment in case it caused a heart attack. He failed to specify who was at most risk of the heart attack – Agent Lee, the medic, or Mrs Yeager? Mercifully, the van was equipped with noise-cancelling headphones, and Lee put some on. She relaxed in her seat, comforted by the blissful tones of classical music.

A while later, they reached an area of parkland and approached a large, white building set back from the road. At first sight, it looked similar to any other business park.

'Welcome to Foundation Headquarters,' said Lee.

Mrs Yeager was sure to be making caustic remarks, and Lee chuckled to herself that she could not hear a word. The van pulled into a driveway and approached a gatehouse. Lee showed her pass, and they were waved through. As they drove on, an optical illusion was revealed. The white building was surrounded by a substantial wall and moat, which were hidden from the main road. The van negotiated a steep slope and entered a tunnel where it was sprayed with disinfectant gas. Scanners examined the vehicle for threats while a row of metal bins flashed in unison as they passed by. To Lee's relief, the occupants of the van were recognised, and the sentries did not open fire.

'Here we go,' said Lee, as they emerged into daylight.

The driver pulled up under a covered area, and Lee unlocked the van.

'Everybody out,' said Lee. 'Agent Brown, please escort Mrs Yeager to reception. All other agents are to report to Security.'

The reception area was vast and swarmed with armed guards. Two huge rectangular windows dominated its façade, and daylight streamed in through a tessellated glass roof. A miniature rainforest stood at the centre of the foyer around an artificial waterfall, which was intended to spread a feeling of calm.

'You'll be safe here, Mrs Yeager,' said Lee, taking off her headphones.

'I was supposed to be safe at home. I want to see Cuthbertson immediately! Do you hear?'

The agents on guard eyed the new arrivals and smirked.

'I think the whole country heard you,' said Lee.

'But first, I need a restroom,' said Mrs Yeager.

Lee looked around for someone in charge. What was going on? And why had everyone been summoned to HQ? Mrs Yeager followed Agent Brown across a marble floor to the visitors' area. She refused offers of refreshment and instead used her right index finger to full effect, jabbing at anyone who dared to approach.

'It's okay, madam, this building's impregnable,' said a smiling receptionist.

'Boom!'

An almighty explosion shook the floor like an earthquake and threw everyone off their feet. Windows in the foyer cracked and splintered into jagged shards, held together only by micro-engineering and air pressure.

****

Five floors above, Jenkins felt the building shake and grinned.

'Idiots,' he muttered.

He prepared his weapons for action and ran towards Cuthbertson's office. Jenkins' nerve system blocked all sensations of pain. Miraculously, his gunshot wounds had healed, and his bruises had vanished. Even his cuts were knitting themselves back together. He had never felt more alive. Jenkins sprinted down a carpeted corridor consumed by thoughts of revenge, and minutes from his goal.

****

On the first floor, Greaves hurtled out of the waste chute like a cannonball. He flew headfirst towards the opposite wall and dragged the commando with him. He came to rest with his boots smoking and scorch marks on his trousers and body armour. The commando groaned under his weight and struggled to roll him away.

'You are in *big* trouble!' said the commando, moving Greaves into the recovery position.

****

Brigadier Cuthbertson found a quiet corner of the Control Centre and checked his phone messages. Quark had left several, each sounding more urgent than the last. Apparently, the computer system was now operational, including the satellite links. Quark also had something important he wanted to share face to face. Cuthbertson sent him a reply by text.

'My office in five minutes.'

Cuthbertson excused himself from the Control Centre and hurried to his private office. It held one of only a handful of secure connections in the whole building. With any luck, he would be able to access the satellite network and find out if Krankhausen had been caught. They had exchanged a few text messages, but Reynard seemed rather vague, which was unlike him.

The lifts were out of action, and Cuthbertson was unused to climbing. Halfway up the stairs, he paused to catch his breath. Cuthbertson groaned and resolved to move his office to the first floor. He was getting too old for all this exertion.

'Damn you, Krankhausen!'

He would be having words with Captain Ayres as well. They should have caught Jenkins hours ago. How hard could it be to capture one man? Cuthbertson reached the third floor and was pursued by a junior agent.

'Mrs Yeager wants to see you, sir. She says it's urgent.'

'Stuff and nonsense,' said Cuthbertson. 'That woman can

123

wait!'

No sooner had the words left his lips than an almighty explosion threw him off his feet. He cushioned his fall on his right arm and lay dazed on the stairs for a moment.

'What in blazes was that?'

But the junior agent did not hear a word. He was out cold.

'Never mind, I'll find out myself,' said Cuthbertson, staggering up the final steps.

****

Jenkins reached Cuthbertson's office and melted the door lock with his blaster. The charred remains of the wooden entrance swung inwards.

'See? What did I tell you? Call this secure?'

He recalled advising Cuthbertson to make improvements to HQ's security. But would he listen? Not a chance. Cuthbertson was too busy attending expensive dinners and the opera. Why the Foundation hired Jenkins in the first place was beyond him. It was clear Cuthbertson had no intention of improving the Foundation's security, and now he would suffer for his incompetence.

Jenkins crept inside the room and half expected to find Cuthbertson waiting for him. The office was luxurious and full of antique furniture. It contained stylish lamps, chairs, tables, and even a drinks cabinet. In many respects, it resembled a gentleman's club. Jenkins sat on a leather chair and began to type at Cuthbertson's personal computer. Guessing Cuthbertson's password would be the most challenging part of his plan. He remembered some secret files he had accessed and typed the first thing that came into his head - *Bounder*.

It was the name of Cuthbertson's favourite dog, an ageing Golden Retriever. Incredibly, Cuthbertson had not changed his password in months, and the computer allowed him access.

'Stupid man,' said Jenkins. 'You're going to pay for what

you've done.'

He selected *HQ Building* from a menu and clicked *Site Cleanse*.

'It's time we cleared out the deadwood,' he muttered to himself. 'And I bet you haven't changed the auto-destruct key either?'

Flames again filled his mind. Clara would soon have her revenge. But it would not be served cold. No, he would avenge his sister in a white-hot crater of fusing matter. It was no less than the Foundation deserved.

'Say goodbye, Brigadier,' said Jenkins, as he typed.

CHAPTER 16: TARGET PRACTICE

Reynard stood on the cargo ramp and glared at the trail left by Agent Rusham's TAC. He was joined by the weapons operator and Sergeant Briggs. Skyraptor-one hovered in level flight, a hundred feet above the glistening water. Reynard scanned the deck for weapons, but it was empty apart from a spare TAC.

'Sergeant Briggs, we're going to need your help.'

Briggs jumped to attention.

'Help us to move this TAC to the launch position, will you?'

'Right away, sir!'

The three men dragged the TAC out into daylight. The ramp creaked and groaned under their combined weight.

'Do you think it'll hold, sir?' said Weapons.

'If it can hold a tank, it can easily support us,' said Reynard.

'Quite right, sir,' said Briggs. 'What are you hoping to do?'

'Whatever we can,' said Reynard.

'Look!' said Weapons. In the distance, the nearest of the hydrofoils had turned towards them. A cloud of white smoke covered its deck and was pierced by a trail of flames.

'Missile incoming!' said Reynard into his earpiece.

'Flight, do you have control?'

'No sir, our controls are still locked.'

'Radar? Any signals?'

'Our tracking system is still down, sir.'

'Listen up, crew. We have incoming missiles. Abandon ship! Repeat, abandon ship!'

The missile stayed low in the sky and raced towards them. Reynard realised they had seconds before impact and turned his attention to the weapon mounted on the TAC. It was a Matteract, a crude but effective device. He sat behind it, aimed at the incoming missile, and fired, but nothing happened. Briggs stepped forwards. He flicked a safety catch and gave a thumbs-up.

'Try again, sir. It should be ready any time now.'

The missile swooped in mid-air and thundered ever closer. Against the glistening water, it was difficult to see.

'Where's it gone?' said Reynard.

'One o'clock, sir,' said Weapons.

'I have it.'

Reynard pulled the trigger and prayed. The Matteract hummed and unleashed an invisible beam that vaporised everything in its path.

'Baamm!'

The missile disintegrated, forcing the three men to shield their eyes. Reynard turned back and watched tiny fragments glow and dissolve into thin air. It happened so fast the missile did not have time to detonate.

'Missile, incoming!' said Weapons.

The nearest hydrofoil had fired again was joined by a sister ship. Reynard aimed the Matteract, but this time the missile was high above them and difficult to track.

'Sergeant, where are your men?' said Reynard. 'We need those ships destroyed!'

'I'll hurry them up, sir,' said Briggs, clicking on his earpiece.

Briggs contacted every assault team in turn. One had run out of fuel and ditched, while the other two were circling in range of the hydrofoils. Briggs ordered them to open fire.

The second missile gained height and began a curved descent. From his vantage point, Reynard could only see its exhaust trail. If he fired, he risked hitting the nose cone of his own aircraft.

'Help me undo this thing!' said Reynard, struggling with the weapon's mounting.

'Allow me, sir,' said Briggs, unscrewing two swivel clips.

But the missile had disappeared from view.

'Boom!'

Wreckage from the missile fell from the sky and splashed

into the sea.

'What happened?' said Reynard, wiping his brow.

'Our boys happened! Look, half that ship's gone!' said Briggs, pointing at a smoking wreck where the first hydrofoil had been.

'I'll finish them off!' said Reynard, aiming at the smoke.

'They're too far away, sir. All you'll do is boil the ocean,' said Weapons.

But Reynard ignored him. Sure enough, a cone of steam stretched across the water and stopped well short of the wreck. Reynard cursed.

'They've launched another missile, sir!' said Weapons.

A curved trail of smoke approached from the second hydrofoil. Reynard aimed and fired again. This time the Matteract was silent.

'What's the matter with this thing?'

'You've drained its fuel cell,' said Briggs.

'What else do we have?' said Reynard.

Briggs opened a weapons case on the wall.

'Here catch!' he said, throwing blasters to Reynard and Weapons.

The three men fired repeatedly. However, the missile continued to race towards them unscathed.

'Stand aside, flyboys!' cried a voice behind them.

It was Major Clavity. He staggered forwards balancing a long, rectangular tube on his shoulder and fired. Flames streaked through the cargo deck and narrowly cleared the Raptor's nose.

'What the heck?' cried Reynard, diving for cover.

Clavity stood proudly holding a smoking tube.

'Heat-seeker. Watch her go, boys.'

Sure enough, the heat-seeking missile arced into the sky and sought out the hostile. In a blinding flash, the two missiles exploded above them.

'You could have taken our heads off, Major!' said Reynard.

'Better a few hairs on your head than this whole ship,' said Clavity, smiling. 'Besides, I outrank you, remember?'

Reynard gave a deep scowl.

'Not on this aircraft you don't!'

Briggs received a message on his earpiece.

'TAC Three reports a direct hit on the second hydrofoil, sir.'

'Good work, Sergeant! Send them our thanks,' said Reynard. 'By the way, does anyone know how to fly a Skyraptor?'

'Flight here, sir. Our controls are still locked. We're holding steady at the moment, but I don't know for how much longer.'

'I thought I ordered you to abandon ship?' said Reynard.

'Say again, sir? Your signal's breaking up.'

****

Rusham increased their speed and skimmed a couple of waves before hauling the TAC into level flight.

'How are you doing back there?'

'I'm okay,' said Sean, relieved to still be on board after their sharp descent.

He sheltered behind Rusham to catch his breath and glanced at the sea below. It seemed calm enough, but he was not keen on falling into the cold water. Sean gripped the TAC and kept his head down.

'We've nearly reached our target. I'll give you a countdown. When I get to *one,* pull the trigger, understood?'

'Yes, got it.'

Why Rusham was making such a fuss about pulling a trigger was beyond him. Sean had fired plenty of things at funfairs and arcades.

Rising from the ocean like a gigantic tornado, the waterspout soon dominated their field of vision. It seemed to defy gravity, and the noise it made was deafening. Sean trembled. Rusham slowed and kept one hand on the TAC's throttle.

'Are you ready, Sean?'

'Yes.'

'Standby. In three, two, one, fire!'

Sean unclipped himself and leaned forwards. He gripped the Matteract's stock in his left hand and pulled the trigger with his right. As he did so, his left shoulder knocked against the weapon. Fortunately, the mounting held firm or Rusham would have lost her head.

'Come on, Sean!' said Rusham as the spiralling water loomed ever closer.

With seconds to spare, the Matteract powered up and hummed. Sean strained against the recoil and tried to clip himself back on. However, he missed the D-ring and twisted sideways. Ahead of them, anti-matter struck seawater and vaporised a tunnel through the vortex. Rusham accelerated into the opening, and they swept through a funnel of steam a split-second before it closed.

The inside of the waterspout was eerie, and it rumbled like thunder. Sean wiped condensation from his visor and gripped his legs tight around the TAC's body. He tried to lean forwards, but Rusham banked right and began to circle the platform. Struggling to stay upright, Sean thrust his tether in search of the D-ring and missed.

'Get on there!' he cried.

'I'm trying,' said Rusham. 'Hold on.'

Sean panicked and grabbed the Matteract. He steadied himself and reached for the tether with a gloved hand.

'Come on,' he said through gritted teeth.

'Keep your hair on!' said Rusham, steering sharply to their left.

A sudden jolt knocked the tether against the D-ring and the two connected. Sean fell forwards and gasped for air. Rusham spiralled the TAC down to the main deck and steered to avoid a mangled tower.

'Slow down!' said Sean.

'I'm trying!' said Rusham, jabbing the controls in desperation.

They slowed a little, but their momentum was against

them. Rusham dived steeply towards the platform and headed for a large viewing deck.

'Brace yourself!' said Rusham.

The TAC broke through the remains of a glass wall. Its left-wing cut through a window frame in a shower of sparks which slowed them for a moment. However, the TAC ploughed on towards the floor. At the last second, Rusham raised its nose, and they bounced and skidded across the deck. Their right-wing caught a row of desks and dragged a pile of furniture along with them. The TAC gouged a screeching path across the floor. Sean prayed they would stop before they hit the far wall. Rusham cut its engine and discharged a parachute. A tangle of cord and half-deployed silk caught on a fallen girder. Swinging on the cord, the TAC veered left. It crashed through a door and came to rest wedged between the balustrades of a staircase.

Sean slumped forwards and felt nauseous.

'Nice landing,' he muttered.

'One of my best,' said Rusham.

While they recovered, Sean considered their situation. For all they knew, Krankhausen might have an army on board, and they had landed right in the middle of his base. He shuddered at the thought.

'Hey! Over here!' cried a distant voice.

'Did you hear that?' said Rusham.

'What?' said Sean, unmoved.

Rusham slid off the TAC and reached for her blaster.

'Stay here, Sean. If I don't come back, find somewhere to hide until help arrives.'

'It's okay,' said Sean, 'I think they're leaving.'

Rusham rolled her eyes.

'Yeah, right.'

She crept out into the main deck, leaving Sean to unclip himself.

Easing herself around a shattered door frame, Rusham scanned the deck. Satisfied it was clear, she tiptoed around debris and trod on some broken glass.

'Crack!'

'Kuso!' she whispered.

'Who's there?' said a man's voice.

Rusham knelt behind a large, potted tree and surveyed the deck. It was a vast space, littered with damaged equipment and splinters of glass. The voice came from behind a bank of shattered computer screens.

'Can you cut me down?'

Rusham inched closer and took refuge behind a pile of upended furniture. She reasoned it was probably a trick.

'Please hurry!'

Rusham switched her blaster to stun and crept towards the voice. Wreckage was scattered across the deck, and she used it as cover until the stranger was in sight.

'There's no rush. We've got all the time in the world.'

Convinced she was being watched, Rusham surveyed the room. Beside a rack of equipment stood a thickset man with an ugly face and thinning hair. He was tied to wall brackets, and his wrists were purple. Rusham aimed for his torso and fired, knocking him out with a single shot. She crouched and listened. Aside from the thundering water outside, the deck was quiet. Rusham inched forwards and checked the stranger's limbs. Whoever he was, he was bound securely by his hands and wrists. Krankhausen had left him to his fate. But why?

'Wake up,' said Rusham, slapping the man's face.

'What?' he said, still groggy.

Rusham tried again, and this time he came around.

'Who are you?'

The man groaned.

'Where's Krankhausen?'

'Who?'

'Your boss?'

'I don't know what you're talking about.'

Rusham sighed. She realised they would need a mind probe for this one. He was either stubborn or stupid. She tried a different tack and waved the blaster in front of his face.

'Why has Krankhausen left you dangling here like a piece of meat?'

'Who?' said the man. 'Cut me down, will you?'

Rusham shook her head.

'No way. I know where you've been.'

The stranger gestured towards the outer deck.

'Look outside.'

There was an even louder roar. Rusham turned and watched the upper lip of the vortex fold in on itself. The weight of the falling water became a gigantic wave surging towards them.

'Hold on tight!'

'Sean?' said Rusham, sprinting back across the deck. 'Sean! Grab hold of something! There's a wave coming!'

CHAPTER 17: CODE 96

Cuthbertson panted and wheezed up the final flight of stairs determined to reach his office.

'Ayres, what's going on down there?'

'We've had a gas explosion in the basement, sir. At least four men are hurt. We managed to shut off the mains, or it would have been much worse.'

'Good grief!' said Cuthbertson. 'And where's Jenkins?'

'We're not sure, sir. He was spotted climbing a lift shaft before the explosion. We're searching the building for him now.'

'Find him and take him down! Keep me posted.'

'Will do, sir.'

Cuthbertson drew his blaster and selected rapid fire. If Jenkins was still on the loose, he could be anywhere. Cuthbertson reasoned his state-of-the-art blaster would be more than a match for him.

****

Seawater surged from the shattered viewing gallery and carried a mass of debris into Krankhausen's base. Rusham clambered onto some furniture and was carried upwards by the rising water. Powerless, she clung to floating debris and was buffeted ever higher by the incoming waves. After a few minutes, the surge died down and a strong undercurrent took over, dragging everything with it. Rusham watched desks and tables disappear from view, pulled by the force of the retreating water. Her improvised raft was sure to follow, and she looked around for a means of escape.

'I'm sorry, Sean!' she cried. 'Why did I ever get you into this?'

****

Reynard returned to the flight deck.

'Captain, we have our controls back,' said Flight.

'Excellent, take us to a safe height,' said Reynard.

'But the cargo doors are still locked open, sir.'

'Never mind, take us as high as you can,' said Reynard.

Skyraptor-one rose and circled the remains of Krankhausen's base. Reynard studied the waterspout and noticed life rafts scattered across the sea. Suddenly, the vortex collapsed, and several enormous waves crashed towards them.

'By Ze'us! Warn Deuce and the assault teams there's some heavy surf coming their way.'

'Yes, sir. We have an incoming message from the Founder.'

'Go ahead,' said Reynard.

'Imperative you stop Krankhausen. Use any means necessary. Keep Sean Yeager safe. Recovery craft will arrive soon. Code 96 authorised by Cassius Olandis.'

Reynard shuddered. This was the first time he had received a direct order from the Founder. It also meant the Founder was aware of their mission status, which was worrying.

'Our orders are clear,' said Reynard. 'But *where* are Rusham and Yeager?'

'On that platform,' said Clavity, returning to the flight deck.

Reynard shook his head in disbelief.

'Unbelievable! Then we need to rescue them. Stand-by for recovery work, everyone.'

'But we only have our flight crew left, sir,' said Weapons. 'Everyone else is in the water.'

****

Cuthbertson paused a short distance from his private suite. Something was wrong. He had met no commandos along the corridor, and there was a light shining from his office. He edged nearer and noticed his office door was hanging in charred pieces from its hinges. A faint tapping echoed from inside his office. Someone was using his computer. Jenkins had access to restricted files, which meant he was able to log in to almost any computer. Cuthbertson felt sick. Why had he not realised before?

'He's found the auto-destruct codes!'

Cuthbertson took some slow breaths to calm himself. If Jenkins succeeded, the whole base would be molten within minutes. He considered sending an SOS message but realised it would take too long for help to arrive. It was up to him to stop Jenkins, or thousands of lives would be lost, including his own. He thought about his family and his dog before leaping into action.

'Jenkins!' he cried, charging into his office and firing at the desk.

A screen exploded, and blaster bolts hit the walls and carpet. Jenkins was taken by surprise and ducked, leaving his blaster on the desktop.

'You're too late, Brigadier! Your security is a joke!'

'Give it up, Jenkins! Or I'll secure you in a coffin!' said Cuthbertson, crouching beside a table and waiting for his weapon to recharge.

Jenkins reached for his blaster and fired with his head still under the desk. Shots hit the walls, pictures, and ornaments. By chance, one winged Cuthbertson's right arm.

'Argh!'

Cuthbertson took cover behind a leather armchair, one of three in his treasured collection.

'You'll pay for what you've done!' said Jenkins, as he peppered the chairs with blaster bolts.

Cuthbertson lay as flat as he could on the carpet and used his weaker left hand to hold the blaster. His right arm throbbed and brought tears to his eyes. Shots ripped holes in the walls and shattered his beloved lamps. Cuthbertson noticed his weapon had at last recharged. If he was lucky, he would have one last chance. He crawled forwards and aimed at knee height below the desk. Cuthbertson's blaster erupted, releasing six shots within milliseconds. The first shot sent splinters flying into the air. The second hit Jenkins' blaster and wrenched it from his grasp. Another shot pierced the remains of the computer screen, and the rest struck Jenkins.

'Ahh!' he screamed.

Cuthbertson peered around the shattered desk from a safe distance. Jenkins lay on his back and started to wheeze. He watched in horror as Jenkins' body began to split apart. His trunk split open to reveal small, squid-like creatures that sprang out and leapt across the room. Cuthbertson backed away and shook his blaster, willing it to recharge.

****

A pale man in dark glasses ranted at a bank of screens in a submarine's control room.

'Make them attack!'

'I'm transmitting your orders now, master,' said Seventy-one.

The two figures watched Cuthbertson crouch and aim his weapon. They zoomed in with another camera and filled a second screen with Cuthbertson's anxious face.

'Detonate the first bio-bot!' said Deveraux.

'It will be done, master.'

They watched a squid-like creature explode, sending liquid and gases towards Cuthbertson's body. At the last instant, Cuthbertson turned his back and took the impact on his jacket.

'We have him. Detonate the second!' said Deveraux.

'Priming, master,' said Seventy-one.

In the background, two commandos raced into the room and fired their weapons. Moments later, the screen crackled and went blank.

'We've lost contact with our bio-bots, master.'

'Sha'biosh!' cried Deveraux, taking off his shades to reveal two burning red eyes. 'I tire of this failure. Head for deep water and prepare our prisoner for the Constructor.'

'Yes, master, it will be done,' said Seventy-one, leaving the room.

****

Reynard watched the tidal waves subside and breathed a sigh of relief. A battered collection of life rafts rode out the last ripples. No doubt the commandos were soaking, but at least they were still alive. He touched his earpiece.

'Sergeant, are you ready?'

'Yes, sir. TAC Five is fuelled and ready to fly.'

'Okay, Flight, let's fish out our rescue party. Sergeant, prepare to welcome our lucky volunteers aboard.'

'Yes, sir. I'm preparing the cargo nets now.'

'Captain, three recovery craft are heading our way,' said Comms.

'At last!' said Reynard. 'Tell them to get here as soon as possible.'

'Yes, sir.'

Skyraptor-one approached a cluster of life rafts and hovered above them. Briggs lowered cargo nets into the water and helped four sodden commandos haul themselves onto the loading ramp.

'Enjoy your swim, lads?'

'Very refreshing, Sarge,' said a burly commando, who was dripping from head to toe.

'Right, lads, Captain Reynard needs us to get over to that platform and finish our mission.'

'We've already tried that, Sarge. It was a complete wash-out,' said another commando.

'Seriously, lads, we have a gutsy, young lady and teenager on that heap. Heaven knows if they're alive or dead, but they need our help. Let's show them what Sigma Force can do.'

'Yes, sir!' said the four commandos together.

'Tool up, and prepare for an abseil drop,' said Briggs. 'This time, I'm coming with you.'

The commandos squelched through the Skyraptor in search of weapons and equipment. They scoured every storage compartment they could find and assembled a pile of helmets, gloves, dry clothes, and sidearms.

'Not exactly standard issue, but it will have to do,' said Briggs.

They were joined by Reynard and stood to attention.

'Your mission, gentlemen, is to rescue Rusham and Yeager. And clear Krankhausen's base of enemy personnel, weapons, and any Foundation equipment you find. Any questions?'

'What about the hostiles, sir?' said a commando.

'Take them prisoner if you can. But if they put up a fight, you're authorised to use lethal force,' said Reynard, nodding to Briggs.

'Get ready, lads. Drop time is in five minutes.'

Briggs took Reynard to one side.

'What are your plans for the spare TAC, Captain?'

'I'll come and help if you're caught in a fire-fight,' said Reynard.

'Very good, sir,' said Briggs.

****

Sean sat dazed for a few minutes. The TAC was wedged at an awkward angle, and he needed time to recover after their crash landing. He heard a deafening roar of water and someone shouting. It sounded like Rusham, but her voice was too faint to carry over the din. Sean guessed it was bad news and tried to free himself by unclipping his tether. He tugged in all directions, but it refused to budge. The metal clip was fused solid, and he was chained to the TAC.

Over his shoulder, Sean noticed seawater stream around the broken door. It carried pieces of broken furniture, which gathered behind the TAC's tail. Water cascaded downstairs in a trickle which quickly became a flood. The surge grew more and more powerful until it filled the lower stairwell. Sean felt the TAC rock underneath him, and the strong current began to twist it around. Cold seawater splashed onto his sneakers, and he lifted his feet clear of the waterline.

While he sat pinned to his seat, a long-forgotten memory flashed into Sean's mind. He remembered a seaside trip, hunting for crabs in a tidal pool. He stumbled and wedged his right foot between two jagged rocks near the water's edge. Sean felt a cold tide wash over his socks and tried to move, but his shoe was stuck tight. In a panic, he cried out for help. A familiar man approached, though he could not remember his face. The man reached into the foaming water and untied his shoelace, releasing his foot. At once, Sean felt a sense of relief as he was carried away from the rocks holding a dripping shoe.

'That's it!' thought Sean. What was it his mum always told him? Think laterally.

Rusham had done a great job of tightening his life vest, but after a few seconds, Sean had unbuckled it. He pulled it off and was free, which was just as well because the water had almost reached his seat. Sean discarded the lifejacket and clambered along the middle of the TAC on his hands and knees. He reached its nose cone and caught hold of a stair rail. By levering himself sideways, he managed to vault onto a dry step. Sean hurried up the first few flights and dared not look back until he reached a safe height. Below him, the TAC groaned and screeched before sliding underwater.

'That was close,' he whispered. 'I hope Rusham's okay.'

Sean climbed to a landing and listened. Apart from the roaring of water and creaking metal, there was no sign of any movement.

'Right, what have you done with my Dreampad?' he muttered.

Sean scaled another flight of stairs and reached an upper floor. A light shone from a half-open doorway, and he inched forwards to investigate. He entered a short corridor, which led to a set of glass doors. He slipped through an airlock and entered a white room with curved walls. It resembled a large doctor's surgery, but its windows were darkened. A strong smell of antiseptic hung in the air. Hairs prickled on the back of Sean's neck, and he sensed he was not alone. An examination couch lay on its side among an array of discarded medical equipment. Sean tiptoed around them.

A muffled sound came from an office on his left. He stopped dead in his tracks. His pulse racing, he ducked behind an overturned cabinet.

'Hungry,' said a child-like voice.

A tall, hunched figure staggered across the room and began to pick at some fallen equipment. It wore grey overalls and had a full head of brown hair with smooth, flushed skin. Its face was full and round, like a baby's, and it waddled around uncertainly.

'Want food,' said the gigantic man-child, shuffling into the office.

Sean hurried to another hiding place and peered around a medical trolley. He spotted two figures in the office and noticed they were arguing. The second figure was dressed all in black and was rifling through cupboards and drawers. He turned around, and his eyes flashed red. The giant demanded food, but red-eyes shoved it aside and continued its search.

'Hungry!' cried the giant.

Red-eyes turned and fired two darts at its tormenter, one of which struck an arm or shoulder. Sean was unsure which.

'Hurts! Hurts!' cried the giant as it hobbled out of the office.

Red-eyes filled a bag and emerged from the doorway. It scanned the room, and its eyes glistened like lasers. Sean dropped to his knees and hid behind the trolley. He waited and heard footsteps cross the room. They paused.

'Give me!' cried the giant.

There was a crash of something heavy hitting the floor and a groan. It was followed by more footsteps, which left the room. Sean rose and edged around the debris. The man-child lay on its side mewling, but there was no sign of red-eyes.

Sean stole across the room and hurried inside the office. It was a complete mess. Papers were strewn all over the floor, and drawers were upended. He noticed an upturned lamp and a bowl of fruit on a desk. Something colourful caught his eye. It was a partly concealed comic. He approached the desk and uncovered a familiar-looking page.

'Rise of the Ultrabulous One!' he muttered.

Sean rolled it up and tucked it inside his jacket. He scoured the office for his Dreampad and sifted through the discarded contents of drawers.

'Give food!' cried the giant.

Sean span on his heels. The man-child stood in the doorway. It had a dart stuck in its arm and reached a hand towards him.

'Who you?' slobbered the giant, its jaws wide open.

It appeared to have tiny teeth and spoke like an overgrown toddler. Sean looked around for something to defend himself.

'Want food,' said the creature, staring into Sean's eyes. 'Give me!' it cried, waving its fist.

The giant waddled closer, and Sean backed away behind the desk. He kept the creature at arm's length, but his escape route was blocked. Each time he edged to one side of the desk, the man-child moved to block his path. It pounded a fist on the desktop.

'Hungry!'

'The fruit bowl,' thought Sean. 'I wonder?'

He lunged and grabbed the bowl before backing away. It was a thin wooden dish containing a handful of apples and a battered-looking orange.

'Here,' said Sean, waving an apple. 'What's this?'

The giant slobbered and gazed at the fruit with wide eyes. 'Give me.'

Sean waved the apple in front of him and threw it out of the office door.

'Fetch!'

The creature grunted and scampered after it, bouncing off

the doorframe on its way out. Sean took a deep sigh and continued his search.

'It has to be here somewhere!'

While rummaging through a pile of papers, he came across a photograph of a young man stapled to a list of names. The face seemed familiar. On a printed sheet, he read his name and address. At the top of the page was a title, which read: *Foundation Priority-one Subjects.*

'That's Dad,' whispered Sean.

A shuffling sound disturbed his thoughts.

'Need more!'

Sean hurried back to the desk and selected an orange. This time, the creature caught it in mid-air and bit straight into its peel.

'Yuck! Not like!' it cried and dropped the orange on the floor.

To buy himself more time, Sean hurled another apple over the giant's shoulder. He returned to the photograph and folded it inside a pocket. He was about to search the last drawer when a fog gripped his mind. Three dark eyes fixed him in their gaze, and his thoughts clouded over.

'Feel my pain,' said a deep, soulless voice.

A blinding ache spread through Sean's head. He staggered behind the desk and slumped into a chair. He was vaguely aware of his hands typing while a red mist glazed over his eyes.

'Confirm self-destruct timing,' said the computer.

Sean's hand reached for a mouse and clicked a button.

'Self-destruct in five minutes. Confirm your selection.'

He hesitated and tried to fight back. The dark eyes returned, and a piercing sensation stung the back of his wrist.

'No!' cried Sean.

He watched his hand reach for the *Enter* key and was unable to stop it.

'Need more!'

Something grabbed Sean's arm, and he felt himself being dragged out of the chair. He fell onto the floor. His eyes cleared, and he found the giant looming over him, its face flushed with rage.

'Still hungry!'

Sean looked around for the fruit bowl. It lay several feet away, upside-down and out of reach. The last apple was nowhere to be seen.

'There! Look!' said Sean, pointing.

The giant followed his gaze and spotted the fruit bowl. It lumbered towards it. While the creature tried to pick it up, Sean crawled away. He reached the doorway and staggered to his feet.

'Need more!' cried the giant.

'Sean picked up a discarded metal tray and ran for his life. He had almost reached the outer door when the giant caught him by his jacket. Sean beat it away howling.

'Find something else to eat!'

The creature hauled itself up and snarled in his direction. It was a pathetic sight, but Sean was determined not to be the next item on its menu.

CHAPTER 18: HOME TRUTHS

Sean raced back to the staircase pursued by the now enraged giant. He considered his options. He could climb higher in the hope of hiding on an upper deck or take his chances in the floodwater below. Something told him swimming was a better choice, and Sean descended as fast as he could. He raced down the stairs, half sliding on the handrail, and reached the lower deck. The water had subsided, although the stairwell was still flooded. Sean managed to wade across the landing. Up to his knees in cold seawater, he headed for the main deck. The giant followed but hesitated at the water's edge.

'Hungry! Want food!'

From a safe distance, Sean watched the creature dip a naked foot in the water. It flinched.

'Cold!'

It took a faltering step, slipped, and fell. Sean hoped the creature would be frightened, but it jumped up again, spluttering and shaking its head. The creature reminded him of a freakish monster and not the kind you would want to take home.

The main deck was now peaceful. Water dripped from the walls, and most of the furniture had gone. Sean headed for the viewing gallery in the hope of finding a way out. Wading through the water was hard work, and he was soon out of breath.

'It's gaining on you! Hurry!' cried a voice from above.

Sean looked up and saw Rusham nestled on a roof girder.

'Can't you shoot it?'

Rusham shook her head and turned out her pockets.

'I've lost my blaster. Head to the outer deck!'

The creature waded towards him with its hands stretched out.

'Want food now!'

'Up here, you big gorilla!' cried Rusham.

The giant stopped for a moment, unsure of what to do.

'Here, catch!' said Rusham, snapping a flare stick and letting it go.

It landed in the water in a brilliant red blaze. The creature stepped back, covered its face, and screamed. While the flare hissed and burned itself out, Sean took refuge behind a heap of fallen metalwork and scanned the deck. His exit was blocked by debris piled up on the inside of the viewing deck.

A familiar howl of engines echoed around them.

Several black lines fell through the roof and splashed into the water.

'Go, team! Go!' cried a voice.

Seconds later, four commandos arrived at speed and stopped just above the waterline to unclip themselves.

'Need food!' said the creature, wading towards the nearest.

It was stopped in its tracks by a stun-shot and collapsed to its knees.

'Where's, Sean?' said Briggs, eyeing Rusham with a bemused look.

'Over here!' cried a commando.

Briggs detached a grappling hook and line from his webbing and threw it over Rusham's girder. It looped in the air, caught the metal spar, and span around it.

'Come on down, m'lady, we've no time to hang around. I take it you can abseil?'

Rusham grunted and began to inch her way down the line.

'It's about time you turned up.'

Meanwhile, Sean accepted a commando's help and allowed himself to be fitted into a harness.

'What about my Dreampad?'

'My job is to keep you alive, son,' said the commando, giving a thumbs-up. 'Happy landings.'

Sean felt the harness dig into his body, and the next second, he was weightless. He passed through the remains of the damaged roof and dangled above Krankhausen's base. Eager hands hauled him on board Skyraptor-one and onto his feet. Sean stepped out of the harness and was surprised to be hugged by Major Clavity.

'Welcome back, big guy. I'm glad to see you in one piece.'

Sean took a step back.

'Yeah, okay. Steady.'

****

Cuthbertson was badly hurt, but thanks to medication, he only felt a little light-headed. He sat in a blue medical gown on the edge of a hospital bed.

'I just need to make a quick call, Doctor. I won't be long.'

The doctor smiled and wrote some notes on a clipboard. He gestured to a nurse who nodded and inspected an injector cartridge. Cuthbertson dialled a number.

'Reynard here, sir. How can I help you?'

'What's your mission status, Captain?'

'We've recovered Rusham and Yeager, and we've searched Krankhausen's base.'

'Any sign of him?'

'None, sir. But we've taken two prisoners.'

'Have you found the Matteract?'

'No, sir. There's no trace of it.'

'Okay, Captain, carry out Code 96. We don't want any awkward questions from our international partners.'

'Right away, sir. We're charging up the cannons now. By the way, the recovery craft have arrived. They've started to lift Deuce.'

'Very good, Captain. Carry on. Over and out.'

As he spoke, the nurse touched the injector cartridge to his neck. Cuthbertson folded sideways onto the bed. The doctor sighed and removed the phone from Cuthbertson's grasp before handing it to the nurse.

'Sleep well, Brigadier,' he said, lifting his legs onto the bed.

Cuthbertson rested in the Foundation Medical Centre for several days. His shoulder and neck were heavily bandaged, and he slept off the effects of a major operation. Two strangers dressed as orderlies entered his private room. They scanned from floor to ceiling and closed the blinds. Once they were sure everything was in order, one of them spoke into watch. The men drew weapons from inside their coats and took up positions beside the door and bed. They were joined by a tall, slim figure dressed in a grey trench coat. The figure approached the bed and put his hands gently on either side of Cuthbertson's temples. He closed his pale grey eyes as if meditating.

'Wake,' he whispered.

Cuthbertson stirred and sat upright.

'I wasn't expecting you, sir,' said Cuthbertson, becoming agitated.

'Relax, Henry. You can call me Cassius. I hear you've had a challenging couple of days?'

'I can only apologise, sir.'

Olandis walked slowly around the bed and pulled up a plastic chair. As he did so, he studied Cuthbertson's face and smiled. He leaned towards a vase of flowers and took in their scent.

'Why are you so worried, Henry?'

Cuthbertson released a deep breath.

'It's all been such a mess, sir. What with the damage and everything.'

'Yes, I can remember some dark days. April 1815 and June 1908 were particularly difficult. We live in troubled times, Henry.'

'Are you relieving me of command?' said Cuthbertson.

'Good grief no, Henry! I didn't recruit you from the Army to drop you at the first sign of trouble. Your team has done remarkably well in the circumstances.'

Cuthbertson looked confused. Krankhausen had escaped, a Matteract was lost, and the Foundation's headquarters had been seriously damaged. He was unsure whether to believe his ears or resign on the spot.

'My dear, Henry, it is I who should be apologising. And I

think I owe you an explanation,' said Olandis.

Cuthbertson was uncertain what to say. Instead, he waited for Olandis to speak.

'Several months ago, we were approached by several governments and asked to shut down Krankhausen's operation. Since we prefer to keep our partners on good terms, we agreed.'

Cuthbertson's eyes widened. He knew the Foundation cooperated with governments around the world, but why had he not been informed?

'So we laid some bait to expose Krankhausen.'

'Sean Yeager?' said Cuthbertson.

'Actually, no. It was Jenkins.'

Cuthbertson was surprised.

'So why have we been protecting the Yeager boy all this time?'

Olandis was silent for a moment as if choosing his words. He glanced at the ceiling and drew a long breath.

'Because, Henry, Sean is an asset. One day he'll join the Foundation, and we must do everything we can to protect our future generations.'

'I see,' said Cuthbertson, unconvinced. 'But what did Krankhausen want from Jenkins?'

'Information, or so we thought. However, it appears our enemies are more cunning than we anticipated.'

Cuthbertson was taken aback. Had his entire organisation been put at risk simply to catch *one* criminal?

'Ah, my dear Henry, I do believe you're teasing me,' said Olandis.

'About what?' said Cuthbertson, feigning innocence.

'Surely you already know why we took these risks?'

Cuthbertson felt stunned.

'I do?'

Olandis poured a cup of water, and Cuthbertson gratefully accepted it.

'Put simply, Henry, we have enemies. And we've had them for many years.'

Cuthbertson spluttered water onto the bedsheets.

'Krankhausen? But we caught him years ago?'

Olandis shook his head.

'We tracked a craft leaving Krankhausen's base. It was almost certainly Darius Deveraux.'

'Who?' said Cuthbertson, bemused.

'Darius Deveraux is possibly the most dangerous man on this planet.'

Cuthbertson was dumbfounded.

'But where's Krankhausen?'

'Somewhere deep underwater, if he's still alive. We lost track of Deveraux's submarine soon after it left Krankhausen's base.'

Cuthbertson tried to stifle a yawn. Instead, his eyes watered. He felt as if his whole world had collapsed around him, and the past few days had been a bad dream.

'You need rest, Henry. We can talk again later,' said Olandis, rising from his chair. 'By the way, I'll be borrowing Major Clavity for a few months. Oh, and Captain Reynard sends his regards.'

Cuthbertson shrugged at the prospect of losing Clavity. He would be glad if Clavity left the Foundation altogether. Reynard, on the other hand, was a good man.

'And one last thing, we need to reward Agent Rusham,' said Olandis, putting his chair back in place.

'What for? She put the entire mission at risk.'

'Henry, if it were not for her actions, we would have lost Sigma Force.'

Olandis turned and walked towards the door, followed by his bodyguards.

'Goodbye, Henry. I wish you a speedy recovery. Now, rest.'

Cuthbertson's eyes closed, and he slumped into a deep and relaxing sleep.

****

On Skyraptor-one the mood was buoyant. Its weary crew looked forward to seeing their families again. However, Sean was unusually quiet.

'So much for keeping you safe, Sean. Any chance of you staying at home next time and doing what you're told?' said Clavity.

Sean shook his head.

'It's boring at home.'

'What I don't understand is where Krankhausen disappeared to,' said Rusham, stretching her right arm as high as it would allow.

Clavity shrugged and turned to Sean.

'What do you think?'

Sean stared blankly into space. He was wary of being admonished and still angry about losing his Dreampad.

'Underwater, presumably?' said Clavity.

Sean nodded and looked out of the cabin window.

'I hear you picked up a pet monster, Sean?' said Clavity. 'Some kind of mutant?'

'Don't tease him,' said Rusham. 'He's been through a lot today.'

'It's not his fault,' said Sean. 'He didn't ask to be made. They weren't feeding him properly, that's all.'

'Speaking of which,' said Clavity, handing out two trays of rations. 'Here you go. I bet you could eat a horse?'

Sean took the food and smiled, but Rusham raised her eyebrows in disgust.

'Or mushrooms, if you prefer?' said Clavity. 'Anyway, what happened to the other prisoner?'

'He's in the brig,' said Rusham. 'But he's not talking.'

'Any idea who he is?'

'No, but I think Krankhausen left him behind for a reason,' said Rusham.

'He's dangerous,' said Sean.

'All the more reason to bring him back with us for questioning,' said Clavity.

'Orders are orders, Major. Surely you of all people know

that?' said Rusham.

'I'm just glad you're both back in one piece,' said Clavity.

Sean finished a mouthful of food and licked his lips.

'They only wanted Krankhausen and something from the laboratory.'

'Perhaps they couldn't control the waterspout and attack us at the same time?' said Clavity.

Rusham frowned.

'More likely, they saw the recovery ships and fled. I think we just got lucky.'

'Either way, you're both heroes,' said Clavity.

'Tell that to Reynard,' said Rusham. 'He won't even look me in the eye.'

If this was how heroes felt, Sean was not interested. All he wanted was to return home and get some sleep. If he played his cards right, Sean reasoned his mother would buy him a new Dreampad. However, the rest of his belongings were irreplaceable. He checked the comic tucked inside his jacket and felt a sense of relief. At least he still had *one* of the comics his father had left him.

Agent Rusham looked quizzical.

'Don't worry about it. He'll come around,' said Clavity. 'And Reynard still owes you dinner, doesn't he?'

Rusham scowled.

****

Professor Quark hobbled into Cuthbertson's private ward carrying a bottle. Cuthbertson noticed that Quark's nose and chin were covered in plasters.

'What happened to you, Professor?'

'I tried balancing a blazing fire door on my face. I wouldn't recommend it as a party trick.'

Cuthbertson laughed.

'So who's running things while I'm shackled in here?'

'Captain Ayres and Agent Lee, I believe,' said Quark. 'But I don't think we'll be hearing wedding bells anytime soon.'

Cuthbertson frowned.

'It's okay, Henry, I'm keeping an eye on them,' said Quark, with a grin.

Cuthbertson noticed the bottle in Quark's hand and nodded mischievously.

'I offer a trade,' said Quark. 'This fine vintage for a substantially increased budget.'

'You strike a hard bargain, Professor. I'll see what I can do,' said Cuthbertson, reaching for a cup. 'By the way, what in heaven's name happened to Jenkins?'

Quark pushed his glasses further up his plastered nose.

'That's a very good question, Henry. We're not sure.'

Cuthbertson looked surprised.

'Haven't you carried out an autopsy?'

'We've examined his remains. But to be honest, Henry, we've never seen anything like it.'

'What do you mean?'

Quark cleared his throat.

'Jenkins wasn't entirely human. His body was a collection of symbiotic organisms inside a human shell.'

'Are you referring to those squid things?'

'Yes. We examined Jenkins' body, but there wasn't much left of him. My guess is the squid were engineered specially to attack. Of course, one of them exploded right in front of you.'

'Exploded? How?' said Cuthbertson.

'By igniting a mixture of organic gases,' said Quark. 'By the way, we found traces of acid and venom on your uniform. You're lucky to be alive.'

Cuthbertson paled.

'Was Jenkins always carrying those creatures?'

'We don't think so. Judging by the scar tissue in his body, we believe Jenkins was altered organically from the inside. Probably after being infected.'

'And he thought the Foundation had killed his sister?'

Quark nodded.

'Whoever did this to Jenkins needed his appearance to

remain unchanged. They brainwashed him and directed him to cause as much damage as possible.'

Cuthbertson winced.

'Poor man.'

'Indeed.'

Cuthbertson had so many questions, but he struggled to find the right words in his drowsy condition. The effects of his operation were beginning to catch up on him.

'I expect you want to know about Sean Yeager and the prisoners?' said Quark.

'Another time, Professor. But please don't let any of them out of your sight?'

Quark walked to the door and offered a brief wave of his hand.

'I'll keep an eye on things,' he said. 'And I'll visit you again tomorrow.'

****

It was a few hours after touchdown, and Sean was fast asleep in the back of a chauffeur-driven limousine. Rusham sat beside him with Mrs Yeager, who was relieved to see her son again.

'Where are you taking us?' said Mrs Yeager, in a calm voice. 'I thought we were going home?'

Rusham gave a faint smile.

'The Founder insisted that we moved you both to a safe house. We're concerned about the burglars coming back. The Founder sends his thanks and best wishes.'

'But what about our belongings?'

'They've already been packed and moved,' said Rusham. 'I think you'll be pleasantly surprised.'

Mrs Yeager looked unconvinced as they drove along a narrow lane and approached a large, walled building and a gatehouse. A guard in plainclothes appeared and scanned the car.

'It's a hotel!' said Mrs Yeager. 'You're going to make us

live in a hotel?'

Rusham smiled.

'Actually, the entire house is for you and Sean. And your staff, of course.'

Mrs Yeager was speechless. She peered out at an elegant, stately home and glanced at Rusham, who nodded reassuringly.

'Oh, and before I forget, Major Clavity wants Sean to have this,' said Rusham.

Mrs Yeager accepted a chunky watch.

'It's a small gift. We didn't manage to recover any of Sean's belongings.'

'Thanks. And how are you?' said Mrs Yeager, noticing Rusham's bandaged wrist.

'I'll be fine. It's only a sprain. They're promoting me to Sigma Squad.'

'Please be honest with me, are we in danger?' said Mrs Yeager, staring deep into Rusham's eyes.

Rusham gave a faint smile.

'We believe Krankhausen is dead, and the team here will protect you twenty-four hours a day. This is only a precaution, Mrs Yeager.'

Sarah Yeager nodded. It was the same well-rehearsed story she had heard many times before. But when would it end?

****

Greerbo sat on a bare mattress in an isolation cell deep inside Foundation HQ. He twitched slightly and sneezed. His head began to throb, and he lay down to rest. Visions of destruction filled his mind, and he let out a groan. Greerbo's body began to sweat and cramp.

CHAPTER 19: EVIDENCE

When the mind upload had finally ended, Deijan Klesus rolled over in his chair and groaned. He reached for an energy tonic and gulped it down. Klesus felt exhausted and far too old for his punishing regime.

'Next time, 12-59, can you just show me the highlights?'

'Affirmative, those were the highlights,' said the spy-bot. 'Would you like to review more information?'

'No thanks. Next time, only tell me what I need to know.'

Klesus' brain struggled to interpret the vast amount of data he had received. He felt a migraine coming on, and he knew it would be days until his thoughts would clear again.

'What information do you require?' said 12-59.

'Show me this unusual DNA,' said Klesus.

A holographic display filled the centre of his living quarters. In mid-air, colourful DNA molecules and clumps of broken spirals floated in three dimensions.

'We gathered data from Sean Yeager's samples,' said 12-59.

'Alviqua, display a comparison of these fragments with Aenaid genes,' said Klesus.

A kaleidoscope of rounded shapes formed spirals and staircases in front of him. The spirals overlapped, becoming one in all but a few places.

'We have a 92% match, Deijan,' said Alviqua. 'All the unique Aenaid base pairs are present.'

Klesus rubbed his temples. In his stressed condition, it was a struggle to think straight. He drank more tonic and considered his next question.

'Who were the parents of this subject?'

There was silence for a moment while the sentient computer prepared its answer. Klesus took another sip of tonic. With any luck, it would wake him up or send him into a deep sleep. He didn't care which.

'We found insufficient evidence to confirm the parents of this subject,' said 12-59.

Klesus raised his eyebrows in frustration. Another useless answer.

'Show me the design of this Matteract.'

A blueprint appeared alongside an image of a Matteract. It opened to reveal the devices working parts in three dimensions. Klesus was impressed.

'And who invented this device?'

'We found no evidence to confirm the inventor,' said 12-59.

'Oh, come on!' said Klesus. 'What have you been doing all this time?'

'Please clarify your question,' said 12-59.

'Forget it,' said Klesus. 'Confirm the origins of the lifeform known as Darius Deveraux.

'Darius Deveraux is confirmed as a hybrid humanoid.'

'Hybrid from what sources?' said Klesus.

'A human and an unknown life form,' said 12-59.

'Let me guess; you found insufficient evidence to confirm the nature of the other life form?'

'Affirmative,' said 12-59.

Klesus sighed. It was clear something unusual was happening on Terra Prime, but obtaining reliable facts about the anomalies was proving difficult. The situation reminded him of reading ancient Terran newspapers when he was a student. They were full of half-truths, distractions, and outright lies. At the time, it occurred to him that Terrans were the most accomplished liars in the galaxy, which was quite an achievement given the youthfulness of their race.

'Take a wild guess, 12-59, what other life form gave genes to this Darius Deveraux?'

'We have insufficient evidence to determine…'

'I see,' said Klesus. 'So why didn't you take samples of Deveraux's DNA?'

'Deijan, we tried to obtain samples, but our probe was detected and destroyed,' said Alviqua.

This was a puzzling situation. It was unusual for Aenaid probes to be detected, let alone destroyed.

'Alviqua, I have made my decision.'

'I am ready to receive your orders, Deijan,' said the computer.

'Send another scout ship to Terra Prime. If it finds an Aenaid colony there, I want them brought back to Aenathen Omega for debriefing. And find the commander of the first scout ship. I want to know exactly what happened to his mission.'

Alviqua considered his orders for several long seconds.

'It will be done, Deijan.'

'I also want to know more about this Darius Deveraux and the inventor of the Matteract.'

'Thank you for your orders, Deijan. It will be done,' said Alviqua.

Klesus staggered to his sleeping quarters. He hoped to relax for at least a few hours.

'Sentients!' he muttered, his mind still racing.

Klesus reached for another glass of tonic. In his fragile heart, he knew it would not be long until he was woken again.

The End
(of the first adventure)

Read on for an excerpt from:
Sean Yeager Hunters Hunted

Thank you *for reading this story. We hope you have enjoyed it. If you have, please tell your friends and family about Sean Yeager Adventures.* **And please post a review on Amazon, Goodreads, or a similar site to introduce new readers to the series Every review helps us to publish new SYA books.**

Sean Yeager *continues his quest for answers in Hunters Hunted. Rumour has it, Sean meets a new friend and goes in search of a mysterious treasure while Darius Deveraux carries out his evil plan. But you didn't hear anything from us, okay?*

For more information *about Sean Yeager's world, visit:*

www.SeanYeager.com

Available in sequence:

Sean Yeager and the DNA Thief
Sean Yeager Hunters Hunted
Sean Yeager Claws of Time
Sean Yeager Mortal Thread

HUNTERS HUNTED:
PARKING TROUBLE

Hughes joined a four-lane road lined by trees. Vehicles passed on either side, but the traffic was light for a Saturday morning.

'Where to now?'

'Turn right at the end,' said Stafford. 'The mall is just a few blocks away.'

Sean felt a shiver run through his spine.

'Someone's following us.'

'Yeah, about half of Yeatsford,' said Hughes.

'There's nothing on our scope,' said Stafford.

A car exploded on their left and careered into the air. Hughes swerved to avoid it and accelerated away. Stafford spotted three flying shapes on the rearview camera. They skimmed above the traffic and fired a volley of energy bolts.

'Hostiles detected. Take evasive action,' said Pegasus.

'Burn rubber!' said Stafford.

'I'm trying,' said Hughes.

'Hurry, man! They're gaining.'

'Is there any chance of you shooting back?' said Hughes.

'Pegasus, activate manual cannons,' said Stafford, pulling a control pad from the glove box.

Hughes gunned the engine and weaved around slower traffic. Pegasus raced past a speed camera which flashed for a second before bursting into flames.

'Darn it!' said Stafford.

'You sure roasted that speed camera,' said Hughes.

'Never mind your speeding ticket. Get us to the mall!'

Hughes took a sharp right and threw his passengers sideways. An energy bolt skimmed their roof and incinerated a nearby tree.

'Can't we just fly out of here?' said Sean.

'No,' said Stafford. 'We're not allowed to fly in built-up areas.'

'Even in an emergency?' said Hughes.

'You're not trained. And I could lose my job.'

Sean glanced out of the rear window. He counted six flying craft split into two groups. Their pilots knelt forwards on small, black machines and were difficult to see against the gloomy sky.

'Boom!'

A passing van rolled onto its roof. Hughes steered around it, screeching all four wheels.

'They're gaining on us!' said Hughes.

A cannon blast from Pegasus hit one of the hostile craft. It swerved into the back of a double-decker bus, and its pilot crashed through an upstairs window. He landed face-down on a seat and lay there dazed for a moment. Meanwhile, the passengers did their best to ignore the dark-suited intruder, as if his sudden arrival was somehow a regular occurrence. A ticket inspector arrived.

'Hey, mate, have you got a ticket?'

The androbot righted itself, ran back down the aisle, and jumped out of the broken window headfirst. It somersaulted in mid-air, dented a car roof, and sprinted away after its colleagues.

'Young people today...' said an elderly passenger.

Pegasus accelerated around a corner and under a concrete bridge. Two hostiles had almost caught up, but they misjudged their speed. One flew over the bridge and crashed into an office block. The second scraped under the bridge and tore into a row of orange ceiling lights. Its pilot was unseated and rolled down the road while the craft bounced and exploded.

'In there,' said Stafford, pointing at an entrance labelled: 'Staff only'.

Hughes smashed through a barrier and headed for a row of illuminated glass doors at one end of the mall.

'Where now?' said Hughes.

'Inside!' said Stafford.

Pegasus mounted a curb and skidded to a halt. As it did so, a man wearing a fluorescent bib appeared and gestured towards them.

'Hey, you can't park here! This is a staff car park!'

Stafford hauled Sean out of the car.

'I meant *through* the doors.'

'Call me squeamish, but I'm not into head-on collisions,' said Hughes, turning off the engine.

The parking attendant blocked Stafford's path and jabbed his finger at Pegasus.

'I need you to move your vehicle *this instant,* or I'm calling the Police.'

Stafford brushed him aside.

'Go ahead. And while you're at it, tell the Police about *them!*'

A group of androbots had gathered at the entrance to the car park like a gang of bikers. They spread out to block the road.

'Pegasus, auto-protect system on,' said Stafford, ushering Sean towards the shopping centre.

'Armed and ready,' said Pegasus.

The parking attendant took one look at the hovering androbots and began to jab his finger in their direction. However, before he could say a word, the air was full of energy bolts and missiles. The exchange was brief and brutal. The androbots fired and missed, shattering the doors to the shopping mall. In return, Pegasus unleashed a volley of heat-seeking missiles and plasma bolts. It destroyed three androbots and numerous cars. The remaining androbots scattered and launched an aerial bombardment. Energy bolts struck Pegasus on its roof and exposed side. It was thrown against the curb and rolled over a line of concrete bollards. Pegasus smashed through a plate-glass window and came to rest lying upside down in the shopping mall. Meanwhile, the parking attendant crawled away on his hands and knees to the sound of car alarms. The staff car park resembled a war zone.

****

Quark's team was busy inspecting cars in the vehicle pound.

'Professor, they've all been sabotaged,' said a technician.

'Impossible!' said Cuthbertson, brushing Quark aside and marching past a line of vehicles.

Cuthbertson climbed into his sports car and slammed the door. He started up its engine. It gave a brief clunk and died. When Cuthbertson tried to get out, he discovered the door was locked tight. Enraged, he thumped on the driver's window but struggled to be heard. A short while later, Quark's phone rang.

'Quark here.'

'It's Cuthbertson. I'm stuck in my infernal car!'

'So, it *is* possible?'

'Get me out of here, Quark!'

'I'll be right with you, sir.'

While Cuthbertson waited to be rescued, a voice spoke on an emergency intercom channel.

'Control, this is Stafford. We are under attack! Send help immediately!'

Cuthbertson tried to join the call, but none of the car's controls would respond. He resorted to using his phone and ordered Captain Ayres to report to the vehicle pound. Meanwhile, Quark arrived with a technician.

'I'll need welding gear; we'll have to cut him out,' said the technician, hurrying away to the stores.

Ayres arrived accompanied by three burly commandos.

'Reporting as ordered, Professor. Where's the Brigadier?'

'He's on a phone conference,' said Quark. 'Follow me.'

Quark led the commandos to the far end of the car park. He opened a sliding door and switched on ceiling lights to reveal an expanse of storage space. On one side stood a row of machines covered in heavy tarpaulins. Quark unveiled one.

'We have a team of agents caught up in a fire-fight at Yeatsford shopping centre, and I need your men to help them.'

'Sure, no problem,' said Ayres. 'Fleet can fly us over there in minutes.'

Quark shook his head.

'I wish we could. Skyraptor-one is on a mission, and Skyraptor-two is being repaired. Our Hoverlifters are too vulnerable, and our Hyperjets are on their way back from Redoubt Island.'

'What about the carpool?' said Ayres.

'Immobilized. Every single vehicle has been sabotaged,' said Quark.

'So, tell me about this...*bike*, Professor?'

'We discovered them last year in a deep storage facility.'

Ayres and his men crowded around the strange machine. It looked like a cross between a motorbike and a snowmobile, except it had no wheels. A long, swept seat met a triangular cross-section, and a fluted skid ran along its underside. A flattened, conical nose and windshield protected the rider, while two exhaust grilles extended from its rear. The vehicle stood upright, covered by a thin layer of dust.

'What is it?' said Ayres.

'This is a Glidebike,' said Quark.

'And how does it work?'

'We looked for a manual in the archives. All we could find was this.'

Quark handed Ayres a frayed sheet of paper. Printed on one side was a single sentence.

'Activate the mind link by gripping the handles and placing your right thumb on the touch plate.'

Ayres eyed the machine with suspicion.

'Do we know what it's capable of?'

'Not really,' said Quark. 'We considered testing one several years ago, but it was never a priority.'

'And who's involved in this fire-fight, Professor?'

'Nine agents and one guard. The hostiles seem to be after

Sean Yeager.'

'*Again*? What is it with that kid?' said Ayres, shaking his head in disbelief.

Quark tapped his nose.

'All I can tell you is that Sean Yeager is very important to our mission.'

Ayres took a deep breath and glanced at the faces of his men. They each nodded.

'Alright, we'll do it. Squad, fetch your body armour and weapons on the double.'

'Yes, sir!' said the commandos, hurrying away.

When his men had departed, Ayres turned to Quark.

'Are these going to work, Professor?'

'Of course,' said Quark. 'All it will take is a little focus.'

****

While Hughes covered their retreat, Stafford pulled Sean through a crowd of shoppers. Alarms rang out from the far end of the shopping mall, and security staff brandishing walkie-talkies hurried to investigate. Inside the mall, shoppers milled around like herds of sheep, oblivious to the drama outside.

'In here,' said Stafford, heading for a department store.

'What's your plan?' said Hughes.

'To stay alive long enough to be rescued,' said Stafford.

'What about *them*?' said Sean, indicating the shoppers.

'Best worry about your own skin,' said Hughes. 'Come on.'

The trio entered a ground-floor cosmetics department and weaved through a maze of glitzy display cases.

'Doof!'

A shelf of perfume bottles erupted beside them, drenching customers and shop assistants in a noxious cocktail of scent and glass.

'Let's scram!' said Hughes. 'This place stinks.'

Another detonation threw eyeliner and blusher into the air, covering passers-by in black and red dye. Customers screamed and fled deeper into the store.

'Upstairs,' said Stafford.

Sean and Hughes waded through a sea of shoppers and reached a deserted escalator. It sat motionless, blocked by a chain barrier and a sign which read: 'Out of order'. Sean unclipped the barrier and scampered up the metal steps, trailed by Stafford and Hughes. Another blast struck a display stand and covered shoppers in shards of crockery.

'Control, we could use some help over here,' said Stafford into his earpiece.

'Agent Stafford, your backup team is engaged in a fire-fight close to your current location.'

'Then tell them to get a move on!'

An energy bolt struck the escalator a few steps below him. It melted a hole the size of a beach ball into the escalator shaft. Stafford hurried up the last few steps and pulled out his sidearm.

'Hughes, get over here! We need to hold them off for as long as we can. Sean, see if you can find a fire escape.'

A few customers wandered around upstairs, uncertain whether to leave the store.

'This one's out of order; take the stairs,' said Stafford.

A boy noticed the weapon in Hughes' hand.

'I want one of those!'

'Trust me, kid, you really don't,' said Hughes. 'I'd run off home if I were you.'

'You can put it on your Santa List,' said his father, herding the boy towards the elevators.

For a few minutes, there was calm. Sean discovered a green fire exit sign a short distance away. On his way back, he discovered the sports department and selected a baseball bat, a skateboard and a tube of tennis balls. A shop assistant watched him rip open their packaging.

'And how are you going to pay for those, young man?'

'He'll pay,' said Sean, pointing at Stafford.

The assistant noticed Stafford's weapon and hurried away to find a superior.

Meanwhile, a dark grey figure appeared at the bottom of the escalator. It crouched and fired, melting part of the handrail. Stafford returned fire and struck the androbot's chest. It staggered back, twitching, and a weapon fell from its hands.

'I need you to lie face down on the floor, and spread out your arms!' cried a voice below.

It was a policeman armed with a Taser.

'Don't do it, officer! Run for your life!' cried Stafford.

The androbot raised an empty hand towards the policeman, who seemed puzzled by the gesture.

'This is your final warning. Lie face down on the floor or I'll fire!'

A bolt of blue energy swept from the androbot's wrist and struck the policeman in the midriff. As he fell, he unleashed the Taser. Its wires spiralled through the air and struck a mannequin dressed in a ladies outfit. Its plastic body sparked, and its wig caught fire. Meanwhile, the androbot recovered its weapon and limped out of sight.

****

Darius Deveraux watched a live video stream of the battle from his control room. An infrared camera followed three figures in an empty department store, and he grinned at what he saw.

'Order the androbots to take Yeager alive. Crush the other two; they are of no consequence.'

'Yes, master; it will be done,' said Seventy-one.

****

Without warning, the department store's lights went out. Hughes peered into the gloom.

'I can hear them coming.'

'You're not wrong,' said Stafford. 'Control, where's our nearest exit point?'

'Two hundred yards from your current location. Your phone app will guide you.'

Emergency lights came on, and Stafford spotted Sean crouched between two aisles, his arms full of sports equipment. Stafford crept nearer, and a volley of energy bolts struck the ceiling above him.

'Get out of here, Sean!' cried Stafford, diving for cover.

A dark figure blocked Sean's route to the fire exit. He hurled a tennis ball at its head, and the androbot fired. The tennis ball exploded in a cloud of yellow fluff. Stafford and Hughes moved from aisle to aisle, firing as they went. Around them, toys exploded on all sides. They were surrounded.

Sean rolled the skateboard towards the steady glow of the fire exit and stepped on board. He pushed frantically and readied the baseball bat. He had almost evaded the androbot's grasping hands when it stuck out a leg and sent him sprawling. A blast wave struck the creature, and it fell sideways, flattening a rack of sports shoes.

'Go, Sean! Go!' cried Stafford.

Sean reached the fire escape, smashed a glass cylinder, and forced open a pair of heavy doors. A piercing alarm sounded, and Sean ran out into the daylight. He reached an empty stairwell and hurried down the first flight of steps. An androbot smashed through a window and landed on a lower landing. It wore a reflective visor and black body armour. It brushed broken glass from its overalls and stood watching him.

'Leave me alone; you freak!' said Sean, brandishing his baseball bat.

The androbot raised a hand and exposed a row of tubes in its wrist. It fired a volley of darts, but Sean dodged to one side, and they pinged against the concrete stairs. The androbot shook its head and extended a fingertip to reveal a sharp needle. It beckoned to him, and Sean panicked.

'Now what can I do? Watch, alive.'

The androbot flexed its legs and leapt up the stairs in a

single bound. Sean swung his bat at the creature's chest, but the androbot wrenched it from his grasp and dropped it into the stairwell. Terrified, Sean ran back to the fire escape. More detonations sounded in the toy department, but there was no sign of Stafford or Hughes. The androbot lunged forwards and grabbed Sean's wrist. It raised its needle finger and prepared to stab him in the neck.

'Watch, protect me!' cried Sean.

His watch face span around and fired a flash of red light at the androbot's visor. The laser beam pierced a hole in the androbot's visor. It cradled its head in its hands and let out a scream. Sean's watch spoke.

'Get away from that thing, Sean! This is Captain Ayres; meet me at street level.'

Sean scurried down the stairs as fast as he could. A blaster bolt rang out behind him, and the androbot fell over the handrail.

'Hurry, Sean!' said Stafford, emerging from the shop.

'Where's Hughes?'

'Doing his job.'

At the bottom of the stairs, Sean crashed through another fire escape and ran outside. He was joined by Stafford.

'Exit Point, one hundred feet ahead,' said Stafford's phone.

'This way!'

Two androbot craft appeared at tree height and swooped down to attack. They fired a broadside of energy bolts and devastated a row of shop fronts. Sean hid behind a concrete pillar and waited, trembling.

'Sean! This way!'

Stafford waited beside a green, portable toilet and waved towards him.

'Over here! Run!'

'To a toilet?'

Before Sean could move, an androbot rammed its flying craft into a shop window between him and Stafford. The androbot staggered from the wreckage and raised its weapon.

Stafford aimed his blaster and tried to fire, but nothing happened. In frustration, he threw it at the assailant. The androbot shrugged it off and fired at Stafford's feet.

'Run past it, Sean! You can do it!'

Sean watched the androbot with wary eyes. It aimed an arm and fired. Sean ducked, but he moved too soon. One dart skimmed his left arm, and another struck his right. He staggered and fell on the pavement. Stafford ran from the toilet and lunged at the androbot. Before he could make contact, an energy bolt struck the creature's back, and it collapsed where it stood. Sean lay on the ground beside him.

Stafford came to lying in a puddle of white liquid. A gloved hand reached down and hauled him to his feet. It was Captain Ayres.

'Come on, Staffy. We need to get Sean to a medic.'

'Better late than never.'

'It was just a case of mind over matter. Come on, I need your help.'

They carried Sean to the portable toilet and rested him on a fake toilet seat.

'I'll never get used to these things,' said Stafford.

'Pleasant trip,' said Ayres, closing the door.

Stafford reached up to a hidden cover on the ceiling and slid it to one side. He punched in a code and pressed his thumb on a blue pad.

'Collection port active,' said a male voice. 'Awaiting rescue craft.'

An interior light flashed, and a blast of air pulled them skyward. Stafford passed out. Moments later, he found himself lying on the floor of a Hyperjet. Sean lay beside him, barely breathing.

'Medic!' cried Stafford, raising an arm.

'What have you done to him?' said a figure, kneeling beside him.

'Kept him alive, mostly,' said Stafford, rolling on his side and wincing. 'There's a dart in his arm.'

'Got it. Relax, we'll be at Kimbleton Hall in a couple of

minutes.'

The medic gave Sean an injection and waved smelling salts under his nose. He let out a groan.

'Sean? Can you hear me? Sean?'

Welcome to the world of Sean Yeager. Watch out! There are androbots and sleepers everywhere.

Sean Yeager Hunters Hunted is available now.

.

Printed in Great Britain
by Amazon

84073582R00108